*Extra*ordinary

FRESH FICTION ABOUT EVERYDAY MARVELS

MOONRISE

ISBN 978-0-6459852-9-0

First published in 2024

Typeset and cover design by Michelle Birrell

Revolutionary University Press is an initiative of Revolutionaries to publish the work of emerging and established creatives and thinkers from university places and spaces. One press for all universities.

Moonrise
Meanjin, Australia
www.moonrise.revolutionaries.com.au

Related Titles from Moonrise

Foreword

Extraordinary: Fresh fiction about everyday marvels is a short fiction anthology that is the least bit banal. In over fifty works of realism, fantasy, speculative fiction, horror and parody, this diverse collection asks its reader to grasp the phenomena of life. From a heart-pumping night at the checkout to letters penned for an unrequited love, from finding hope in a bracelet to an arts grad with a unique relationship with her barista, these stories play with the remarkable in the commonplace, beckoning you to realise that around each corner lies the potential for unexpected epiphanies, life-changing events, strangers with gifts, and exceptional new worlds. So… dive in to see what you might find in the extraordinary.

—R.W., S.H. & O.K.

CONTENTS

*Extra*ordinary

Submerge Yourself

*I*t's beautiful down there. Everything is still; time seems to stop. You move in slow motion, delving through the thickness of blue liquid.

A clean wave approaches, the tip beginning to curl into a sculpted arch. You take a breath and submerge yourself under the heap of water. It's quiet. To your right, a girl glides through the body of water, no faster than you. Sunlight pierces through the surface, guiding you upward. You could hold your breath longer, but you break free from the water. Noise floods your ears; water crumbling, people talking, wind howling. With the next wave approaching, joy begins to surge through you. You take a deeper breath, determined to stay under the water for longer. With your lungs full, you dive down. Touching the sand, scooping up a handful, and watching it gently fall between your fingers. Instead of swimming, you allow the wave to roll over you. *Is this what it would feel like to be in space?* Effortless and light. For a moment you feel safe, you are safe. The suns rays reappear, but you resist the temptation to follow them. You decide to swim forward into the large open space, releasing bubbles; you are in control, even at forty-three. How far can you go? *Forever*, you think, but you come up for air.

'Do you open your eyes underwater?' the younger girl next to you asks.

'Yes,' you say, 'always, it's like immersing in a new world every time.'

She smiles. 'I don't. I'm scared of what I might see.'

'What do you think is down there?'

She hesitates, 'I'm not sure … maybe things that should be left undisturbed.'

'Maybe this time will be different,' you offer, your voice gentle.

She smirks and rides a wave into shore. Did I say the right thing? Your words play over in your mind before you realise, you're alone. A wave of anxiety attempts to creep into your thoughts, but you choose to ignore it. You're stronger than fear. You respect the ocean for all it is and what lies beneath. What should be left undisturbed will remain that way. You reach out, creating ripples that dance across the water. You have nowhere to be, and you feel a sense of contentment. As the ocean calms, you lay your head back and close your eyes; your body naturally follows. The sounds around you, soft rustling, gentle swishing, distant echoes, are trustworthy. The sun melts into your skin, warming you like a kiss from a loved one. How can this be real? The elements of nature gift you beauty and life. What did you do to deserve this?

'Ahh … give me the ball, Reece! I swear if you don't give me the ball.' Reece, tall and lanky at fifteen, charges into the water, the ball securely tucked under his arm; he loses his footing and goes face-first into the ocean.

Jenny laughs, bending over with her hands on her knees, pointing at Reece. 'You look like one of those lizards,' she manages through her laughter, 'the ones that run on their back legs.'

Reece chuckles and splashes her with water. 'Hey, look, it's Mum!' He points to a distant figure floating on their back. 'Mum! Hey! Mum!'

You sink into the feeling of serenity when you hear a person shouting, a familiar sound. *Phantom sounds, surely,* you think. You have dealt with these ever since you had your firstborn. In the shower, *is that the baby crying?* Hanging the clothes on the line, *is my boy calling out to me? 'Reece, what is it?'*

'I didn't say anything, Mum.'

You return to the rhythm of the currents, pushing and pulling. It's just you and the ocean; you try to regroup your thoughts.

'Mum.' Reece's voice bubbles up through the water.

'Oh my god … Reece.' You startle. 'Where'd you come from?' You smile with pride, taking in your sun-kissed, healthy boy. 'Is your sister with you?'

'Yeah, she's trying to keep up, the slowpoke.' He points at Jenny, gliding through the water, stroke after stroke, trying to catch up.

'Mum,' Jenny says, slightly out of breath, 'you look so beautiful out here in the water.'

'Aw, darling.'

'Do you want to play beach volleyball with us? We are going to rally up some friends ... if Reece doesn't keep taking off with the ball ...' Jenny side-eyes Reece.

'Actually, darling, I think I'll sit this one out and head up for a shower and a coffee.' You smile. 'You guys enjoy this beautiful ocean.' You cheekily splash Reece and remind him to play fairly. As you head to the shore, satisfied with being ambushed by your babies, you know the ocean will take care of them. 'Open your eyes when you submerge yourself!' you shout back.

'Yeah, okay, Mum ... and remember to use soap when you shower,' Reece smirks.

A Dandelion by Any Other Name

MICHELLE BIRRELL

*T*hey say you never realise what you've lost until it's gone.

I don't know who 'they' are, but *they* can go to hell.

I can't think about what I've lost. It's too hard. Too painful. Instead, I choose to focus on what I can see right now as I lie on the cold earth and the schnick, schnick, schnick of the shovel fills my ears. Trees tower above me; the soft rustle of their leaves whisper secrets … secrets I don't yet understand. I can't see him. He's behind me. I can barely feel my body. The annoying voice of an animated donkey shrieks in my head, *'My legs! My legs! I can't feel my legs!'* Hysteria boils up my throat and escapes through my lips as bubbles of blood.

I'm dying. I know I am.

He thinks I'm already dead.

I've lost so much, and they are telling me it's too late to be grateful. It's too late to appreciate the breath in my lungs and the simple everyday marvel of waking up. After today, I will never wake up again.

No.

I'm not going to think about it.

The bright bloom of a dandelion turns towards the rising sun—towards me. Is it trying to get my attention? Is it trying to tell me it's going to be okay? The point is moot, anyway. I know nothing is going to be okay again. Not for me at least.

Is it my fault? Should I have seen the signs?

No. This is not my fault. It's his. He's to blame.

Not that it matters now.

The bright yellow of the dandelion once again snags my attention. How does it survive? Cut down by lawnmowers, poisoned by weedkillers, dug from the ground by disgruntled gardeners, and yet it lives on, coming back season after season, year after year. The dandelion is a survivor.

So, no montage of the best moments of my life for me, then, huh?

No 'my life flashed before my eyes' in the moments before my death.

Yeah, no. Just random, useless knowledge about a common weed. Facts sprout in my brain, much like the way dandelions sprout from some of the most inhospitable places on earth. The rose I'd tried to grow with its special fertiliser and carefully pH-balanced soil swooned like a regency lady on a fainting couch when I forgot to water it. Meanwhile, the dandelions squeezed through cracks in the concrete and bobbed their technicolour heads like punks at a rave, raising a middle finger to gardeners and greenskeepers all around the world.

The rose is praised for its beauty, but the dandelion is despised for its resilience.

I think I'd rather be a dandelion. Being a rose has done nothing except land me here. As a rose, I'd been admired, but then I was viciously cut before I even had a chance to fully bloom, displayed in a vase and discarded once I'd served my purpose.

Unlike the dandelion, I couldn't survive.

The dandelion hasn't always been so despised. It was once a favoured plant for its healing properties. Dandelions are packed with enough nutrients to heal sailors from the dreaded scurvy—if they'd thought to bring them on board, at least. The dandelion isn't selfish. It chooses to use its deep roots to give back to the soil it's planted in and nourishes the plants around it. Even in death, the dandelion is a source of wonder. The delicate puff of the seed head begs you to make a wish.

But a rose, when it dies, is soon replaced.

The rose, so admired by man, abhors competition. Fighting to attract pollinators, needing space to spread their roots, they're only happy to share the garden with smaller, less important plants. High maintenance. But they couldn't have always been like that, right? How did they survive before man domesticated them? Cultivated, bred, indoctrinated to think they are nothing more than something pretty to look at. Even the famed scent of the rose has been diminished by man's interference. That's what being grown in a hothouse and forced to bloom out of season does to a plant.

Maybe, if he buries me next to the dandelion, fate will be kind to me. Maybe the dandelion will give me new life, bring me back, reincarnate me in its own image. I'd like to be a dandelion. I could live on forever, haunting him.

Each time he cuts me down, just like a dandelion, just like a hydra, I would sprout a new head—following him around for eternity. A living, recurring reminder of what he did.

He rolls my body into the hastily dug grave. The soft, loamy dirt falls on my cheek as I stare up at him. He doesn't even look at me. I'm already forgotten. I'm no longer the beautiful rose he obsessed over. Now, I'm nothing more than an annoyance to be dealt with.

I will forever be an annoyance he needs to deal with.

I *will* be the dandelion.

Dearest Dorothea

MADELYN WHITE

*D*earest Dorothea,

I miss you very much. How is retirement treating you and John? I'm sure you two must have your hands full with the grandchildren. I still remember seeing Rebecca and John's marriage notice in the papers, seems like only yesterday. Their kids must be entering their teenage years soon, a handful for their parents as well as you, I'm sure.

I'm writing to you from my porch, watching the neighbourhood children play in the park across the street. Their carefree squeals percolate the autumn evening like birdsong. Every day I watch them engage in a new imaginative game and it reminds me of our childhood. Growing up next door to each other certainly had its advantages. Even our parents could not keep us apart.

Do you remember when we used to play princesses in the garden? You would always demand to be the damsel in distress, and I would have to be the prince to save you from the dragon. We never needed anyone else, you and I—it was us against the world. Even as a child you were always so brave, climbing to the highest branch, coaxing me with encouraging words and praise. Such a precocious individual, you made me feel like I could do anything. We would spend hours together, creating our own magical world. Until your father's sharp voice cut through the air, breaking the spell and pulling you back home. I think of that time often and miss the blissful naivety of our youth.

Thinking of you always,

Majorie

Dearest Thea,

I hope you are well. What are you filling your time with these days?

I'm enjoying my quiet life, though it is lonely at times without visitors. I cannot help but feel I missed out on some big part of life. No children to check in on me or grandchildren to fawn over.

My lovely neighbour Inez dropped by her old DVD player and some films she no longer wanted the other day. I'm not very up with the times in that aspect, I never even figured out how to work a VCR. Luckily her son Peter is very tech-savvy and was able to set it up for me.

I was delighted to see *Romeo and Juliet* was in the pile of discs. Do you remember the night we went to see that at the cinema? We slipped in the back after you flirted with the young man at the ticket booth. Even though I knew it was pretend, I could not help but feel envious at the way you made him smile. I remember feeling like criminals, but you and I were used to sneaking around. We watched in wonder, mesmerised by the forbidden love story. High off the thrill of seeing a film your parents would greatly disapprove of, we snuck our way into the bar just down the street and danced in a place where no one knew our names or our stories. Though we were just teenagers I felt like the world was in our hands then—we were invincible. The beating we both got for staying out late reminded us that this was not the case at all.

I often look back on those days, especially when I see two girls walking down the street, giggling together as if nothing else matters but each other.

Love,

Majorie

My love,

I ran into a friend from our university at the supermarket the other day. James Williams, do you remember him? I always thought he fancied you. Though we both know that did not matter. You and I were far too focused on getting up to mischief together to indulge in any other friendships, though this often left us as outcasts by our peers.

I see moments in my life every day that remind me of that time … of you. The ponds down the road take me back to that winter night we went skinny dipping in the university lake. I was terrified we would get caught, but you assured me that no one would see us. I remember how your blanched skin glowed in the moonlight refracting sparkles on the surface of the icy water. Your lips the colour of summer cherries, an enticing red glow I was drawn to in the dark. I remember sneaking back to the dorms, the signs of our rebellion left in puddles of water that dripped from our bodies through the hallway. I remember our stifled giggles as we tumbled into your room, exhilarated by the winter air that stung our naked torsos. I remember everything after that, too … the warden finding us together … the abhorrent words from your father … hysterical cries from your mother. I remember hearing it all through the door, wanting to fight for you as you had always done for me, knowing it would only make it worse.

I think a lot about the years after, but those memories become even more painful. I knew those days could not last forever. After university, the realities of growing up hit us like trucks, for you maybe more so. My memories of the rest of university are marred by your absence.

I cannot find it within myself to forgive your parents for taking you from me. Though I know other forces may have eventually succeeded in the same thing. I know that is most likely the reason these letters go unanswered.

I must tell you that I do not resent you for obliging the wishes of others back then. Those days were harrowing times for us—for people like us. I know in my heart that what we shared was nothing short of remarkable. That people wait lifetimes for even a glimpse of it. I will always love you, Dorothea. As age withers me more each day I will continue to look for you. In the smiles on children's faces, the songs on the radio and the winter breezes. I respect your decision to leave us behind and will stop reaching for you. But I will not stop marvelling in the memories of us and what could have been.

Yours always,
Majorie

The Bear

Emma Clark

*J*f it's brown, lay down. If it's black, fight back. If it's white, goodnight. A measurement of danger on the basis of this animal's black fur is running rampant through my head. Its black eyes reflect my battered face and matted hair as I dig my nails into the dirt underneath me. It's a scene that could only be conjured from someone's nightmare. A campsite littered with claw marks, deserted by people who fled in the darkness of night, who I thought loved me most. I scrunch my eyes shut, feeling its hot breath brush against my face, and I turn my attention to the static and beating heart that clouds my thoughts, trying helplessly to block out the dominating chuffs of the bear that looms above.

Despite my attempts at remaining silent, the shivers that make their way through my body rack out a strangled cry. The bear responds, shifting its weight to its back legs as I watch its bared teeth open to rip out a guttural roar. I see its front paws coming down on me, and my body decides its fate.

Fight.

With clenched fists I push myself up, scraping my knees amongst the brush and finding my way to a wobbly stance. The bear stands almost a metre taller, seemingly mocking me as it too sways side to side. Its silhouette glows as the fire crackles from behind it, encasing me with its shadow. Stumbling back, I bump into a table behind me. I sort through the equipment I'd once thought allowed me to survive. My fingers rejoice in the sting of cold metal, flicking on the torch and pointing it into the eyes of the bear. It swats at the light as I watch its hind legs stagger, stamping its foot into the flames of the fire. Embers and ash explode into the air and drift away without me into the safety of the night sky. My eyes sting at the stink of singeing skin.

The bear claws at itself, its fur catching alight. Ripping at its flesh, the fur falls away. A slimy substance secretes from underneath its layer of hair to show me its face. What I see lying beneath makes my stomach twist in agony.

It's human.

'Get away from me,' I sob, seeing the monster limp towards me, shedding fur like dead skin. It's smaller now, shrinking with each stumbled step. 'Please,' I whisper, 'please stop.' The torch shakes in my hands, its beam erratic.

'You know who I am, Ursel,' it gurgles, wiping grime off their arms.

I see it. The shape of its nose. The green eyes. The matted blonde hair with a face splattered in mud.

It's *me*.

'No,' I choke, 'this isn't real, this can't be real.' My heart feels as though it's been squeezed into fragments. Every sob feels as though the pieces are being tossed within my chest, piercing the delicate lining of what is left inside me. It burns.

'I'm real,' she whispers, pulling her shoulders back, 'I'm you, Ursel, and you are me.'

The fire crackles as I frantically shake my head. 'That's not true,' I yell, sinking to my knees. I'm desperate to block out her words, knowing that the truth falls just beyond my reach. She sits across from me, reflecting every flaw and every scar I have tried so desperately to hide. I'm staring into a broken mirror that reflects every fractured piece of me that I had tried to stow away.

My muscles ache, the exhaustion smothering the fleeting adrenaline that once fuelled my fight. A tear dribbles down my cheek, feeling the fear fade in and travel down to my trembling fists.

'It's true,' she says.

'I scared them away,' I breathe. The realisation slips from me. I look around the camp, seeing the blood from shredded connections that once breathed life into my world. Now, I was left to deflate back into the person who had grown up as an outsider, unable to understand others, myself or why I had to be so different.

She tilts her head. 'Yes, you pushed them away. You can continue to blame me as you have done so up until this moment, but I am a piece of you. There is only so long until you realise that.'

'I am nothing like you!' I feel white hot anger bubble up and out through my mouth. 'You're a monster—a vile creature that shouldn't exist.'

'Is that what you think of this part of yourself? Something that repels those close to you, before they can see this is the thing concealed inside of you?' she says as she slinks back. I stalk over to her, grabbing her by the arm. She struggles against my grasp as I drag her towards the fire. Its flames reach out to her, licking against the side of her body, welcoming her to the fate that I pulled her closer to.

'You know the truth, but you refuse to live it.'

I was expecting a flailing fist, or a mess of limbs being flung around, but she only strains against me for a moment, the warm glow showing her lips moving slightly. 'You live a life of denial,' she murmurs. I watch her become blanketed in the fire, disappearing amongst the hues of red and yellow.

I have won, but I now hold on to the uncovered life that I live. It dawns on me as does the sun. It peeks over the tree line to expose the devastation that is left. I will always know, and it will gnaw at my skin until I am left with nothing but a skeleton. The monster will always be inside me, rattling my bones and stripping what remains around the only honest piece of who I am.

I will always be the bear.

Never Say Goodbye

A. LAMONT

```
Search 09-MARCH-2121 to 12-MARCH-2121

Observation Entry 948 [REDACTED] 15:43
Visitation 974
Visitor Miss [Smith]
Patient [REDACTED]
Observer [Skye]
09-MARCH-2121
```

*C*hair legs screeched across the polished floors. She winced, giving the camera a look. She did this every time. Every time she would haul that oversized chair next to the bed. Every time she recalibrated the neuro link for wireless operation. And every time she asked if we could leave it like that. For next time. We always gave her a smile. Every time, she knew, that might have been the last time.

She curled up in the plush chair, contemplating the neuro link. It always took her a moment to put it on. To activate it. Some days, she never would. Instead, she would only link their hands together and sit. Their breaths the

only sound in the room. One harsh and rattling, one soft
and shuddering.

```
Start [Cloud] Upload 34 [REDACTED] 16:03
Observer Integration 'Successful'
```

The sun was scorching. The sand was hot, the rocks were
hot, and they were barefoot. Unbothered, delighted. Skin
would not burn here in [the cloud]. He stood on the
furthest rocks where the waves broke, dotting his skin with
shards of cool relief.

She stood on the shoreline. A smile on her face, head
tipped towards the sky. The rockpools sprawled before her.
A maze. An obstacle course. A treasure trove. She knew,
ordinarily, they would get lost amongst its wonders. They
would laugh at the skittering crabs, slipping and sliding as
they tried to catch one. Trying to pinch it just right so those
claws would miss them. They would play with the anemone
and stumble through pronouncing anemone. Stumble all
the way into saying it wrong and silly over and over until
it really wasn't funny anymore. Their cheeks would hurt
anyway.

So many little things to marvel at, little worlds to
discover. They would oh and ah until their fingers and toes
wrinkled and their skin felt tight with salt and sun.

But she knew, ordinarily, they wouldn't be in [the
cloud]. Ordinarily, they'd really be here. Walking along the
rocks as easily as you or I would walk down the street. They
were masters of moss and algae. That was years ago.

She looked towards him, silhouetted against the
horizon. It was time.

She stood beside him, heart racing. The rocks were the precipice of his world. She squinted at the glittery turmoil of turquoise. Salt coated her lips.

'Whatcha doing?' She tilted her head at him. He was younger here. His hair was long again, the thick dark waves escaped the tuck behind his ears. The smile lines were still there, crinkling beside his eyes. The freckles and sunspots dotted his skin. She could see the swirl of gold and green and brown of his eyes. All the little details she was terrified of forgetting. Terrified of being replaced with what lay in the hospital bed.

'I am tired.' A frown creased his brow, the hairs unruly. 'But I can't leave you. Why am I worrying about leaving you?'

Back in the room her fingers tightened around his. She closed her eyes, shuddering through a heavy lung of salty air. She felt the ghost of bony knuckles in her fingers. Here her hands curled, for a moment, tightening on air.

'It's time to go,' she whispered. The wind whipped the words away. A wave crashed against the rocks. The spray should've been a relief, instead she shivered. 'It's time for you to go.' She opened her eyes, glistening like the sea before her, she met his gaze. Still, only the waves wet her cheeks. 'I'm gonna be okay.' A couple of greys could be seen in his hairline. Reality was bleeding into [the cloud], it was destabilising.

He shook his head. 'I am meant to look after you. I am meant to watch you grow old. To get married and have children—'

'You can't!' Her breath caught. 'You can't. Not like this. Please. Stop. You're suffering.'

His breath slowed, laboured.

'I am going to miss you every day, at every big moment, and all the little ones in between. But I know you'll be there with me, in my heart, in spirit, in memory.'

He started to lose weight before her eyes, colour drained from his face. We had warned her this might happen again. She didn't react.

'I am going to be okay. I promise. I will see you again, one day.' Tears burned through the salt on her cheeks. She grabbed him then, wrapping her arms around him, and buried her face in his chest. 'Please, promise me you will let go. You don't need to hold on anymore.'

His arms wrapped around her, and his chest stopped beneath her cheek. She counted the seconds. A choking gasp, and the rattling breath reverberated through her. She counted the seconds. He gurgled. She counted. A normal breath. His body began to fill out beneath her arms. [The cloud] was attempting to stabilise.

He whispered, 'I'm sorry. I'm so sorry.'

```
End [Cloud] Upload 34 [REDACTED] 17:07
Observer Separation 'Successful'
```

She returned from the neuro link on a choked sob.

'We apologise for the intrusion, Miss [Smith].' She aimed a puffy glare at the intercom. '[The cloud] failed to stabilise. We understand this may be distressing and have credited your account for the session. Additional funds have been provided—'

'Thank you,' she sniffled. 'I understand the procedure, [Skye].'

'Very well, Miss [Smith].'

She dropped her head onto their entwined hands. And she stayed that way until we sent her home. Their breaths had been the only sound in the room. One harsh and rattling, one soft and shuddering.

```
Observation File Closed
No Further Entries for Patient [REDACTED]
10-MARCH-2121
```

```
        Request Generated 21-MARCH-2121 07:34
```

Madame LaLaurie

MADISON COVENEY

A thousand eyes gaze upon the host's daughters as they are announced down the mahogany staircase, its opulent banister gleaming below the polished chandelier above. Madame Marie LaLaurie, New Orleans' sanctimonious socialite, brushes her brunette hair back ostentatiously, pleased with their descent. She examines the remainder of the ballroom in search of her husband, realising he is nowhere in sight to share the admiration. He knows the occasion is crucial to their daughters' betrothal, their ongoing livelihood, and fortune.

She taps her wine glass with an engraved silver teaspoon, 'Unfortunately, my husband seems to have fallen ill within his bowels. Let this not disturb our celebration, our …' Madame swallows. Quickly, censuring: 'Help, have jorums for refills.' The room halts in consternation, eyeing off the slaves with dark complexions. Borquita strains as her vitiligo-like skin darkens, risking her mask. *You are here for your twin, Bastian,* she reminds herself. *What's the hex again?*

'Ecarnruter,' she mumbles, casting her complexion to bleach back to its false composure.

'Master LaLaurie shall return in health shortly.'

The band inadvertently resumes an upbeat tune, eschewing the underlying unease present and assuring Borquita's cover. The guests' meandering chatter continues, and Madame promptly escapes the hubbub.

She wanders in worry, hoping no one has discovered her husband, or his 'illness'. If she remains in charge of their grandeur, and receives regular blood batches, her husband could fornicate with whomever he fancies. But of course, no one could ever learn of his 'bowel issue', as she likes to refer it. The exposure of such aberration would ensure the fall of her fruition, even insurrection of her draining chamber. Madame LaLaurie's obsession with beauty and power takes great precedence over her husband's betrayal, even if it requires murder.

Madame LaLaurie enters the billiard room beaming like she spotted the Devil dissecting demons. Master LaLaurie frantically pulls his drawers up. Bastian—an emaciated houseslave—bends backward, wiping his mouth. The gossiping downstairs drifts through the halls. Madame LaLaurie's head shoots like a shuttlecock between the traitors. She secures the door, shutting out the chaotic din and shutting in the shameful truth.

'You fool! Why this occasion?' She scolds Master LaLaurie as he tidies his attire.

'And *you*. Despicable moor! You shall pay with your life.'

'Indeed … You shall die kneeling; you seemingly enjoy it.' Master LaLaurie abnegates, snatching a candlestick from a cabinet. He lunges at Bastian, nipping his chin with the candlestick. Bastian struggles against Master LaLaurie on the drugget, but it proves useless. Any possible protest is muffled by the ceremony, punctuating Bastian's fate. The couple, concealed in a facade of civility, drag him through the labyrinthine corridors and down into the threshold of their draining chamber.

Madame LaLaurie, with a steel-cold stare, gestures for Master LaLaurie to restrain Bastian to the far end of the dungeon. She holds her candlelight beside her head, highlighting each besieged slave groaning, while awaiting her next 'kill and refill'. The flickering light cast dancing shadows on the faces of the dead and barely breathing. Their eyes vacant yet filled with unspeakable anguish. Master LaLaurie successfully chains Bastian up, slightly trembling whilst stepping back and searching Madame's face for approval.

'Go back to the party. Ensure our guests are entertained,' she orders.

Without hesitation, Master LaLaurie abandons his mistress, leaving her to commit her ritual. The clinking of chains mingle with the moans of deprived souls—a symphony of despair that reverberates into the air as he exits.

Borquita ululates in her bedroom, her heart heavy in the absence of her twin. His aura was lost last night at the mansion before she could rescue him. Now it is non-existent. In a desperate bid to unravel the mystery shrouding her connection to Bastian, she divulges the ancient art of black magic into her firepit. The ethereal forms of Voodoo spirits materialise before her, vibrating the room with an otherworldly energy. Bastian's tragic fate coruscates in Borquita's mind, igniting a fire of vengeance. The spirits' whispers affirm her resolve, reminding her to confront the malevolence that tore her twin asunder. With the raw power of her magic, Borquita begins weaving incantations, her hands trembling with the weight of her decision. A translucent brew arose from the extinguishing lime flames, initiating Borquita's quest for revenge.

Borquita knells the LaLaurie Crest doorknocker, awaiting strife. Madame LaLaurie cringes as they meet eyes, outlining her wrinkled flaws. Borquita grins tacitly, 'Your Master will become satiated … as he once was with you.' The offer of the youth potion hung in the air like a sinister promise, a falsified peace masking the storm brewing beneath the surface.

The lights project a ray of dim scarlet from the chandelier to the stuffed animal matting in the master bedroom. Borquita senses a strong taint in its presence, particularly emanating from below.

'What is this sorcery?' Madame intriguingly rushes Borquita.

'You can have your youth and beauty back … You shan't worry about Master LaLaurie's debauchery.'

'How did you kno—' she stops, refusing to confirm or deny. 'What is it sourced from?'

'Needn't worry, Mada—'

'I must worry! Not even my concoction can regenerate my youth and beauty.'

Madame LaLaurie reaches to her duchess, grasping a bejewelled coffer.

'This is beauty balm, derived from human blood … only fresh, of course. I acquired this batch from some slave I caught forcing himself on my husband, Bas-ti-an, more like Bastard,' she cackles.

With a venomous snarl, Madame LaLaurie leaps towards Borquita, seizing the vial and downing its contents. Her manic intent attempts shattering the bottle on Borquita's head, but as the potent potion took hold, a heavy lethargy descends upon her. Her vision begins to blur, her face sinks in pallor, her coordination languid, leaving her unconscious at Borquita's feet. Borquita laughs as she removes her cloak, dispersing it into a conflagration upon her egress.

'Enjoy immortality, *Madame LaLaurie* … alone.'

Smoke screams from the chimney, chiming in with the cries from the draining chamber.

Sonder

EMILY TREVITHICK

*C*eleste slams the baseball bat repeatedly onto the dog's body. Her freshly manicured nails grasp the metal in a similar way to how she grips her phone when she takes photos of her breakfast. Or the sunset. Or her at-home reformer Pilates workout. A sickening crack echoes throughout the apartment complex. The piñata is a success. An eruption of cheers floods through the kitchen window and out towards me.

One of Celeste's friends hoists the piñata's battered body over his head like it's some trophy at a football game. Next to him, a younger woman rolls her eyes at his antics. I haven't seen her here before, but it seems her arms are permanently glued together as she's yet to unfold them. I imagine that her bright red lips are muttering to the other women, 'Isn't she a little too old for a piñata?'

I must have been right, as a wounded expression forms on Celeste's fully glammed face. Her dismay is quickly replaced with a grin as the stereo's music blasts loudly once again, deafening any of the attendees' snarky remarks.

Normally, I wear headphones when Celeste hosts parties, otherwise the reverberating occupies my ears until the next day like a musical hangover. But tonight, I'm eager to witness how long the façade of Celeste Barclay lasts.

It's hard to see the kitchen floor from the balcony I'm perched on across from her apartment, but it seems there is an abundance of chocolate in the piñata. I'm sure it's some luxury brand that was gifted to her. Most of the decorations or food at her party were probably free. I feel envy poison my words, but I can't help it. It's been ages since I've tasted anything beyond the cheap coffee and days-old pastries the café downstairs throws out after 4 pm.

Like a moth drawn to the flame, Celeste reaches for her phone. I know it's hers because the case is the ugliest shade of green I have ever seen. According to her Instagram, it's the colour of some new album. Her hazel eyes are likely rewatching the piñata video to check it was captured correctly. She always has to have the perfect angle, the perfect shot. You'd think she'd filmed an Oscar-bait film, not a thirty-second story people are going to skip through. Her friend, who recorded the exchange, is reassuring her that it's fine.

Celeste is the only resident in the apartment complex opposite mine whose name I know for certain, but only because of her Instagram. I hear her shriek out her handle when she goes live on social media, which is pretty much every day. I like guessing what hashtag she is going to use. For tonight's special, I can guarantee that *#thirtyandthriving*, *#birthdaygirl* and *#celebratinglife* will make a guest appearance. My phone died hours ago though, so I'll have to wait until tomorrow to charge it at the café.

The party eventually dulls to music and murmurs. Celeste and her friends are once again in front of the photoshoot wall in the living room. I feel sorry for the man who has been forced to take a million different photos of them, all at different angles and with pre-selected filters. Every time someone attempts to announce their departure with an awkward laugh, Celeste grabs their arm and drags them back into the party, her red fingernails like little leeches.

After everyone leaves, Celeste emerges from the bathroom and spends ten minutes in front of the hallway mirror, reapplying lipstick as if each layer is going to hide any flaws on her special night. I notice her mascara has dripped down to her cheeks. She takes out a small tube and glides it feverishly under her eyes, instantly brightening them. The same can't be said for her smile, as it's puckered into a thin line.

My legs are numb from the slouched position I have been in for the last few hours. I need to remember to bring a pillow from now on, although I don't know where I am going to nick one from. The fire escape's metal groans as I ascend the stairs. The gaps in between are wide enough for my entire body to fall through if I make one slight misstep. Plummeting down ten stories isn't my idea of a fun Saturday night. Laughter and drunken-infused giggles trail upwards with me until the silence of the night swallows the noise. I have one more storey to go.

As I step onto the roof, the wind rustles my singlet and hair. It's going to be a cold night. I reach for the door with the words, 'DO NOT OPEN: MAINTENANCE SHED' displayed across it. The door opens with one swift turn of the handle. No one has checked up here in a few years, lucky me.

I think of Celeste's minimalist, white apartment, with the bowls of fruit, recipe books and fresh flowers styled on the gold-marbled counters. I don't have a kitchen or a living room, just a few camping essentials the shelters have donated to me. The light sometimes works, but I have to tap it a few times. There is no shower or a bath, but the rain infiltrates the space easily.

The shed floor is hard against my back, the cement juts into my spine. I guarantee Celeste has never missed a bed sheet or duvet at night. I think of her hazel eyes and the tightly strung, borderline-suffocating ponytail with blonde highlights. She's obsessed with the perfect appearance, the perfect party. The perfect life. I would rather succumb to the cold in here than surround myself with 'friends' that laugh at my existence behind my back.

My mind drifts as I imagine different scenarios if I reach thirty. Will I have as many fake friends as Celeste or even an extravagant apartment? Bitterness and curiosity interweave my dreams and the wind's howl fills the silence from the absence of friends and family.

Ink and Bones

PAIGE WINCEN

*T*he fox's skeleton is dyed soft, pale lavender. Resin flowers cleave open its chest; a stream of red, cut lead rhinestones drips from the cavity.

It's twisted.

Oscillating between life and death.

'The flowers are a critical component,' she says. 'Embedded is its very own antithetical marvel, a reflection of our contemporary social conditions.' My flatmate Louise clasps her hands to her chest, looking up at the glittering monstrosity with hearts in her eyes.

'And what might they be?' I ask.

'Beats me,' Louise says, flipping a magenta lock of hair over her shoulder. 'That's just what I wrote in my ekphrasis.'

She seems like she's having a laugh—at everyone. At me. This is the third sculpture she's sold for over ten grand, and I sell books for a living. Hard to believe we're the same age.

I know, coming towards the end of her scholarship with Rhode Royal University, Louise spends most of her days isolated in her art studio, or roving God knows where for her supplies. I suspect she's collecting roadkill.

She works hard. But it's also hard not to hate her. Even just a little.

The university café is bustling with people. We find vacant seats inside, tucked away next to the coffee machine where rhythmic puffs of steam make my face sticky. Louise dumps the contents of her bag over the table—pens, charcoal, lolly wrappers—making herself at home. She opens her sketchbook to a clean page and begins fervently sketching crude caricatures of our barista. *Guess it's my shout.*

I wait in line for Tom to take my order. He serves an elderly woman who says something funny, or Tom laughs anyway. It's a genuine laugh, the kind that shows his dimples.

There's no one behind me, so I get to chat with him while I wait for our drinks. He's stuck on till duty since he shattered his hand yesterday. Says he crashed his bike on the way to work.

He hands me my cup and I trace a fingertip over the scrawling ink on the side, accompanied by a smiley face: *Gemma.* Sharp pangs constrict my chest. *Typical Tom. Always smiling.*

Louise sits at the table, ripping an empty sugar sachet into tiny pieces as she awaits my verdict.

'They broke up,' I say. 'She moved out yesterday.'

Her lips twist with a suppressed smile. 'Was it bad? Is he really torn up about it? I bet he's not. He was so out of her league—'

'He's fine,' I cut in before she talks herself into a tirade. 'He's sad, but … he'll be okay.'

A few things I've learned about Tom in our recent visits: He turned 24 last month. He celebrated with his girlfriend—sorry, ex-girlfriend. He doesn't drink coffee; he prefers the oolong his grandma buys for him.

I can't count the number of times I've pried into the love life of our beloved barista. Louise has this almost compulsive need to see him every day; to know what he's been up to, where he goes, and what he likes. Not that she has ever spoken to him. She could never humiliate herself by asking these things herself. *That's like, so desperate*, she would say. So, of course, I do it for her. Because I'm her only friend—as she is mine.

'Right!' Louise slams her cup down on the table and I jump. 'I need to get back to the studio. Finals deadline is a'coming.'

I place my own empty cup down. 'I thought you had ages to do it.'

'I do. But I've just gotten some crazy good inspiration for my next piece. I need to start gathering materials.'

Louise starts swiping scattered pens and charcoal into her bag, along with the ripped sugar sachet.

'Have fun collecting roadkill,' I call as she guns it out of the café.

Louise waves a hand behind her back. 'You know I will.'

I didn't hear from Louise for a week, which is not unusual. She tends to disappear whenever she has a big project due, opting to sleep in her studio rather than come home. I thought about texting her, but I didn't want to break her 'flow'.

Then this morning—three days before her deadline—I get a simple yet loaded text message: My studio. NOW.

At least she's not dead.

The whole tram ride over I wonder what monstrosity could make Louise go awol for this long. The girl has a chronic attachment to her phone, so it must be big.

I consider stopping at the café for a couple takeaways, but when I get close to the door, Tom isn't there. *Weird. Did he break his other hand or something?*

When I enter Louise's studio, she's sitting back on her hands in the centre of the white room walled with erratic charcoal sketches. Her hair is a mess, her eyes glazed over. I take tentative steps toward her, the hollow sound of my shoes against vinyl sends a chill down my spine.

The *thing* in front of us ... Bones, bleach-white and meticulously arranged, form the foundation; a grotesque amalgamation that mimics a figure both human and monstrous. Interwoven are her trademark wildflowers, their colours vivid against the cold, pale surface. They seem to writhe and contort in unnatural ways.

It's revolting. Yet I'm captivated by its intricacy, how it appears so real. Its skeletal mouth frozen in a silent scream, delicate bony fingers clawing at the air, and the texture—

I freeze, eyes fixed on the up-reaching hand, on the jagged lines fracturing the porcelain bone—real, human bone. And etched against the ivory grooves in black ink, a crude imitation of handwriting I'd come to know so well: *Louise.*

My sharp gasp echoes in the silence.

Louise's voice is haunting as she whispers, 'Isn't he beautiful?'

Birdsong

BROOKE EVERISS

*T*he butcher birds had always been there. Their sweet trilling chorused in a melodic cacophony each early morning as the sun burned golden against brown-green trees. They carried with it routine.

That routine ends with your graduation. Those twelve-plus years of sitting hunched at a desk are supposed to mean something, celebrated with applause. Your friends are glad to be rid of high school. You were never going to be good in a trade—your next logical option is university.

'You should move as far away as you can,' your best friend says one night as you both mull over cheap wine and stale chips. 'Get away from your helicopter parents.'

You laugh in agreement.

You get into the second university of your choice with a scholarship. You signed a form and were guaranteed a spot.

To the bright, bustling city full of blaring cars and pretentious academics. A cramped apartment with a bony mattress. To mouldy curtains and no air conditioning in the middle of summer. There's construction outside, almost constantly—new pavements, or townhouses, or filling in potholes on the street. There's no birdsong here.

The classes aren't what you expect. The huge lecture halls are daunting and impersonal. The professors are aloof, hard to talk to.

One girl sits next to you a few times. Mia. Mara? You don't ask a second time. You spend most of your hours staring at your papers until the numbers begin to swirl off the pages.

The silence creeps in slowly, unexpectedly. A stalking cat, hidden until its teeth are sinking through your downy feathers.

At first, it's just a day here or there. You don't need to go to class today; you can follow along in your textbooks. Eventually, it becomes easier to not look altogether. The mornings slip away in a blur of muted alarms and drawn blinds.

Do you need to go grocery shopping this week? You can last until next payday. You should really wash your bedsheets. It's been a week, two, then a month. The apartment feels unlived in. Dark apart from the light that tries to peek under the blinds. Quiet apart from the monotonous spinning of the low-level ceiling fan.

Your phone buzzes. It's on the nightstand. The yawning gap between your mattress and the bedside table stretches between you, an aching chasm that saps your strength as you fight to reach your phone.

Mum, is lit up in a green inbox and a text appears on the screen.

You okay? Haven't heard from you in a while. Give me a call when you can x

Your thumb hovers over the keyboard. The cursor blinks tauntingly, its existence a mockery of words you can't say.

The phone slumps to the mattress. You watch as it slides over the curved edge and listen to its muffled clatter as it hits the carpet.

You roll over.

A shrilly recorded pop song screeches from under the bed. The phone is ringing. Ringing. *Ringing.*

You don't answer. The song ends.

The fan whirs. Outside, a car revs.

The pop song returns. It reverberates from the carpet below, needy and urgent.

Your phone rings. Rings. And rings. Rings until it dies.

It might be an hour later. A day. Three? The effort it takes to drag yourself to the edge of the bed leaves your arms shaking. Your phone buzzes when you charge it.

There are several voicemails, all soft and hesitant. Your mother's voice cracks slightly in the last one.

'Hi sweetheart,' says the message, 'just checking in again. Call me when you get a chance.' There's a pause. The unsaid *I'm worried about you* is thick in the silence. You're almost glad she didn't say it, saving you from a patronising cliche, but a small part of you wants to hear it. Wants to know she's noticed something's off, wrong, broken. 'Love you,' Mum says instead, and the voicemail ends.

You never answer.

The professors here cycle through their students like they're workers at a mass-producing factory checking for faulty products. You're not even a cog in a system. You're *a spare screw thrown into the packaging that nobody ever needs.*

47

The world outside shrinks until it is nothing more than a blurred backdrop.

Something stirs you one day. You're not sure what it is until there's a second, sharper knock at your door.

'It's Maya,' comes a voice from the other side. 'I noticed you haven't been to class in a while.' What class do you share with Maya? You can see her face in your mind. 'Just wanted to check in… Are you okay? You might not even be home, huh?'

Your throat is tight. Some metal band has been strapped around it, welded into your burning skin, squeezing any words that might've wanted to escape. Get up. Open the door. How hard is that, really? *Move.*

'I'm here if you need to talk,' Maya adds after a long pause. Then, quietly, 'We miss you in class.'

The sound of footsteps retreats. The silence returns. It's thicker than before. Choking.

The first cool breath of autumn slips through the window, cracked open just an inch to let in some air. It whispers onto your face, soft and coaxing. Fresh.

Something possesses you, then, and you drag yourself up from the mattress like pulling yourself out from under a thick layer of snow. Swinging your legs over the side of the bed feels like leaping off a cliff.

Outside, the world is moving on without you. The distant rumble of cars, the faint voices of people going about their day.

You stand at your window and hesitate. Light flickers under the blind, grasping, begging to be let in. The blinds pull open and early morning light spills gratefully into the neglected room.

The world outside is still there. That loud, bustling city. Grumbling cars and passing people. The construction has stopped; the new pavement is white and fresh on the street.

A butcher bird trills.

When the World Ends

S.G. Lambert

1.27am Tuesday the world will end. Tomorrow, according to the news, the government alerts, and the radio. They made an unimaginable error, nothing could be done; it was inevitable.

*W*hen was the last time I saw a sunrise? The last opportunity passed and I didn't even know. It's silly but it hurts. It rose in the east with its heat bending over the curvature of the Earth and casting the ocean alight like a million shards of glass. It would have painted the sky purple, bleeding into the night and drowning the stars in its light. Then it would've turned pink and red and orange. We'll all be dead in a matter of hours. And I missed it.

After all that saving and scraping by, we'll never have that holiday in Melbourne. We'll never see Tokyo. I'll never fit into those jeans. I'll never get that tattoo. It's over. There's no time to prepare. It's too late.

'Get comfortable, seek out friends and family, and spend your last moments wisely.'

The dull smash of my favourite mug punctuates the newscaster's drone. The tea sloshes over socked feet and bleeds where tile meets carpet. Get comfortable. *Get comfortable?* That's it? That's all they can say? How the fuck did they miss a meteorite hurtling towards the earth?!

Jarvis calls within minutes.

'Did you hear?' his voice rasps down the line. I squeeze aching eyes shut.

'Yes.'

'I'm on my way home.' He's rushing, throwing things into the back of his ute without care. I can hear each heft, each clatter of a prized possession, all useless now.

'Drive safe.' A habit. He chokes on a laugh before the call ends.

Shock slides into an aching numbness. Like something's been taken away and all that's left is a crater. Yawning and blackened. Bottomless and eery. Gone. Gone. Gone.

Mrs Draton next door waves her arms about and screams. I hear her from the kitchen window, erratic and furious, smashing prized china and sobbing. Tinkerbell yowls, but Mr Draton stays quiet.

Jarvis finds me sitting in the puddle of my tea. Feet and bottom dampened by its cold creep. His steel-capped boots crush the remnants of the mug. He slides down the kitchen island to rest beside me. We hold each other together. My eyes sting but the tears don't come.

We answer call after call from friends and family. Each dull buzz of our phones jolts our pretzeled forms, forcing us to unwind again just to hear and say the same things: *I love you. It was nice knowing you. I'm with family. I'm with friends. I'm sorry I can't be there. You're too far away. It's ok. It'll be ok. Take it easy. I love you.'*

After a while, the time between calls stretch into long bouts of quiet. I don't know when, but we gravitate to the porch. The swinging couch lulling. Dirtied canvas rough and chains squeaking with each rocking motion.

Jarvis's ute is freshly dented on the driver's side door. He shakes his head when I ask, his lack of anger sprouting goosebumps across my sweaty skin.

Magpies warble from the macadamia tree in the front yard. Across the street, the kids play in the sprinkler, school uniforms still on, while their family trickles in under the cream Queenslander. We watch them hug, cry, and share a beer; we wave. We watch them gather on the lawn to point to the sky; we don't look. We don't speak for a long time.

'I'm sorry I didn't do the dishes last night,' Jarvis breaks the silence. It's the first time he's really looked at me since he got home. He grasps my face in both calloused hands. He's so pretty. Something in my chest squeezes.

'It doesn't matter now,' I shrug with a sad smile; my lip wobbles.

'But it did,' he whispers, pressing our foreheads together. And I cry for the softness of it, and because it did and I wish it still would.

The whispered 'I love yous' feel weightier. I think about how I want those to be the last words I say to him, now that I have the choice.

The sun sets and I'm grateful for it. To watch the colours seep into the open sky, setting it alight with pink and orange and red and purple. Jarvis sniffles and I hold him tighter. He's still in his work uniform. Mud caked into the fabric of his knees. I watch his freckled cheeks glow under the setting sun, eyes glassy.

'I didn't love living that much anyway,' I try to joke. His eyes crinkle, blue and bright.

'Yeah,' he snorts.

'I just thought I had more time, ya know?'

'Yeah.'

We stay there, curled around each other. Hands clasped despite the sweat. Kookaburras have their last word before the streetlights come on. The breeze is cool when the frogs start their chirping. Our breaths are out of sync but it's the same muggy air. This is getting comfortable.

Intermittently, updates run on the news, the glow of the TV screen flickers behind the flyscreen. The usually cheery voice of the reporter morphing into a low rasp. She stops telling us of the uproar, of the violence elsewhere, of the last-ditch efforts, shifting to the weather and what planets we'll see in the night sky. At 6pm, the screens go dark for good. Newscasters, cameramen, lighting technicians go home and leave the rest of us in silence.

The street's lit long into the night. Like herded cattle, we emerge onto the street: Jarvis and I, then the Dratons next door with Tinkerbell curled into their embrace, the Smiths and all their relatives across the street, and Bill from down the road. The soft scuff of slippers and pad of bare feet echoes with breaths coming in sighs; we wait.

It ends like New Year's, a countdown, a final kiss and unimaginable light. When the world ends, it's quiet.

Grounded

JAI HEINER-WRIGHT

*F*rom the window of her Queenslander, Sera saw the rocket launch and begin to claw its way into the heavens.

'There'll be plenty of space up there for a couple of cats like us.'

Baptiste yawned, stretched and squeaked in the darkness beside her. The moggy no longer hid during a departure. He simply glanced at the disappearing licks of flame before jumping from the nook onto the bed, patiently staring at his human. Bap's message was clear: The night is cold, so come sleep. Sera sighed and crept under the covers, trying not to disturb her roommate, Marceline. Like a mirage, the ship had vanished.

Sera worked the conveyor belt, a museum exhibit customers skipped past to use the Pay-or-Stay system. She idly watched the aisles of produce as the 'ink' on the price tags squirmed like swarming then scattering ants. Smart paper allowed the company to adjust their prices according to what margins they could grab at that precise moment. Judging by the cost of an elderly man's bananas, cyclone

Marge had finally reached Northern Queensland. His head recoiled at the receipt.

'I spent 150 dollars. Doesn't that mean I get a ticket with this?'

'Sorry, sir, we've run out for today.'

The customer sent her to *the back*. He would expect some time to be spent looking for a replacement roll, so she found a good wall to lean against. As she counted down from 60, Sera fingered his ticket in her smock. Each slip of polymer prints out of her sales terminal. Before handing it to the customer, Sera could use her thumbnail to covertly pry the scratch-away surface up slightly. Often, she would see the corner of a coupon for a free whatever. Every other year though, there would be the glint of a Mars-bound rocket embossed in gold. If she extended her index finger now, she would feel the coolness of that embossing. But she was hesitant to do so. That cold dredged the question: Why am I still taking these?

The draw made her feel like her lungs had never been bigger. It became pleasurable to breathe in deeply. To push against Bap who lay atop her chest. To linger for some time in that contraction until there came a twinge of pain only to empty it out and begin anew. Sera's house had become a den of roommates; Innocents that Marceline had recruited to support their campaign against the 'market-adjusted' rent increase that would come with the lease renewal. The joint allowed her to feel like there was none of this – nothing, in fact – outside her room. There was only her and the warmth of Marceline's hand. Only her and the solidity of Baptiste.

Sera whispered, 'Did I ever tell you about the first time I got high?'

'Yes… no.'

'I was 16, so I still lived with Aubrey. You know how she despised the stuff cause of my addict dad but you, Kayden, Ross were all having fun smoking it. So, I asked Kayden for some of his dad's stuff.'

'Didn't his dad have medical grade?'

'Yeah.'

'Fuck, on your first time too.'

'I thought perhaps it had been laced with something because shit made it hard to breathe. I nearly went to Aubrey for help, but another voice froze me in place. It said I just needed to ride it out. So, I curled up and tried to. But with my head to my knees, I couldn't get rid of the idea that I was spiralling into myself, forever inwards.'

'Like that old Ito manga.'

'Exactly. I didn't think it would ever end. Until there was Bap, a smudge of black back then. He nestled against me, and I looked at him and he looked at me and that inwards spiral disappeared. It became a line between us that I held onto until the body high subsided.'

'Fuck… So, that scared you straight?'

'I *never* touched weed again.'

The roommates watched the smoke that wafted from their joint. Trying to reach the sky, it clawed against the ceiling and destroyed itself in doing so. Sera told Marceline that she got another golden ticket. How she obtained it was said in the uneasy silence.

'You must have your seven by now—'

Sera braced for it.

'-but, Sera, you know you can't take Bap with you.'

She knew. On the day that section of the T&C changed a month ago, it seemed like all her housemates had lined up outside her door. To express condolence, argue it was an injustice and shuffle away. Sera couldn't hear them after a while. They were reduced to whispers against her thoughts. *He'll never know why I left. We speak to each other – that line is there – but there is no language that will allow him to understand this, allow me to justify myself. He'll wait in our room. He'll watch the door every day.* Marceline felt this turmoil through her own line to Sera. She didn't push the subject on the day. But since then, in her sympathetic gaze, in her nervous hand movements, in conversations cut short was her promise that they would return to it. Marceline was a good friend in that way.

'Do you still *want* to go?'

'Sure. Can't let the C-suite have all the fun.'

Are you sure? The question radiated from Marceline's eyes with an intensity that made Sera turn away. There was an inertia that came with these make-believe things: inflation, rent, Mars. After time, they gained enough momentum to justify their own existence; 'I have been therefore I should be.' And Sera had begun watching those rockets many, many years ago. Perhaps, she could nip at that inertia though. Throw doubts in its way until one day, she would be in disbelief that such an unwieldy idea ever had movement at all.

She could start with a small question.

'Do you think I could sell the tickets?'

The Amulet

MITCHELL ARCHER

*T*remors—I know not from my own poxy flesh or ascending through subterranean caverns – disrupted my fragile sleep. Clothes hung from my skin like a serpent that had failed ecdysis. Rivulets of sweat spilled across my scales, intersecting like Rubicons. The dreams had already departed on horseback.

In another room, the amulet beckoned. I had taken especial care to wrap the delicate thread around my frayed knot of a neck afore bed, or so I thought. Memories collide headfirst at high speed, spraying the wreckage of remembrance across my mind's backroads. At least lately.

I dragged my feet across the disjointed floorboards to the kitchenette. The blood in my legs no longer flowed like in days of yore; it coagulated and occasionally sputtered. Extracting the substance would reveal an unholy fusion of phlegm, bile and pus.

Doctor Saklas had said insomnia infects the circadian rhythm via regret. But I have no cause for such: I had been a strict disciplinarian, a providing guardian and a confident lover. Even my final syzygy—which had been a war of attrition from the beginning—expired amicably. I had been tempted to salt their Carthaginian heart, but the amulet had paralysed my arbiting hands.

I live alone now. That is, except for the amulet. I have wondered whether prying neighbours or the authorities who encircle my abode like an ouroboros know that it resides here. The night I had secured the amulet had been one of apocalyptic weather, corrosive mist spraying from the guillotined neck of the heavens. The sky had been an unsettling crimson that night, blotched with dilated clouds. Indeed, it had felt like a million eyes stalking my panicked limp across the courtyard to the maw of my house.

Under the murky glass face of the amulet had swirled bloodred and black; a miniature of the firmament above. Later that evening the colours had drained to an underbelly pink with grey veins and by the morning the glass had thickened to subsume all colour.

In the kitchenette I contemplated the basement door which floated in its frame, stigmataed by splinters to the flaking paint. The dusty digital clock read 2:52am. An hour in which morgues heaved with cadavers and corpses. Since the red night of two Junes ago I had only ventured down the ramshackle stairs twice.

Once, the amulet had been an impenetrable obsidian and was too heavy to lift from the desk in Excaliburian fashion. The second time the teardrop face had been a whirlwind of images, and the amulet had vibrated and jumped so intensely it had sliced new chiromantic lines into my palms. Aside from those episodes, I had only witnessed a palette of alluring colours emanating through the doorframe, but my curiosity had been overwhelmed by my fear.

A chiaroscuro of azure and ultramarine was seeping under the door like the blood of Bluebeard's bride. From my earliest reminiscences to my current senescence blue had represented safety, solitude, slumber. How many hours in my youth had been wasted in an abyss of oceanic dreams? My life had become an unceasing somnambulance. I needed sleep.

And so I stumbled down the stairwell like a centaur pierced by a fatal javelin. Each tendril of blue coiled around an atrophied atom of my body. Mannequins of clutter occupied every square inch of floor, obscuring the desk on which the amulet sat from my gaze. The cerulean beams of light seemed to intensify with each ricochet off a junkpile, creating a mirrormaze.

I saw myself in the shimmering reflection and was disgusted even by my canonised form. Zero vices, no abuse of chemicals, and yet my body was collapsing to supernova. My gangly limbs looking as though they had been snapped at every angle and reattached. And my visage – sunken eyes, mountainous nose and a mangled mouth.

There had been a time when I had tried to be an historian of my own life. To collate the evidence, categorise it and cultivate a sensible narrative. Now all that mattered was the amulet. Knowing it is hidden away in the basement, shifting through shades and murmuring its forbidden language buoyed me with a toxic optimism, a sick health.

Atop the mahogany desk glowed the amulet. I approached it apprehensively, recalling past pains inflicted. I wanted to touch it again; it was not showing its former aposematic façade. The blue was welcoming, much like the melodies of sirens.

Statuesquely, I hesitated. The amulet was my final secret, a mystery to replace the mundanity that defined the epilogue of my life. Prior to my possession of it my life had been empty despite the riches, conquests and abuses. Those had been the formalities of a pathetic existence, insectoid life cycles.

But now this amulet vindicated me. It balanced the scales back to neutrality from the banality of evil and mediocrity. The violently soothing colours were but realigning karmic threads. I had made my peace with never knowing why I had been bestowed this unique favour from the gods.

My withered fingers reached through the blue aura to touch the amulet.

A crow flew over the city, surveying the sprawling ghettoes and neighbourhoods. Its keen eye could see the subtle colour bleeding from each building. From an unassuming house in the outskirts, it saw a blue beam intensify before starting to fade. It swooped.

Friendship Potion

BRYDEE MELICK

*I*t is not often I am called upon. Mostly I just stand on the edge of things and observe. The witches within the coven don't tend to think of me first.

When I arrive at her cobblestone cottage, the Elder Witch is relaxing in a banana chair. Her bony hands are clasped together, her dark knee-length gown is fraying on the ends and her matching pointy hat is askew. What ties it all together is the hot pink flamingo glasses hooked on her crooked nose.

She glances up at me and rises, her hat staying behind. The standard-issue cauldron next to her dwarfs her, as does the loss of her hat. Her dark eyes land on mine and she stares. I gulp.

'I was sent by the—'

'Coven leader, I'm aware.' She dismisses me with a wave and wanders over to a blank wall. 'I asked for a Witchling with potion experience … Is that you?'

'Yes, ma'am.'

'You know, I asked that old woman not to send me any more little helpers, *especially* ones who call me *ma'am*.' The

Witch shoots a glare over her bony shoulder at me. My shoulders drop, and my gaze lands on the floor.

The Witch's cackle sends a cold shiver down my spine. My head snaps back to her.

'And she sends me one with no sense of humour,' she pouts.

I open my mouth to reply but no sound comes out.

'Don't be so uptight, Witchling. Come here.'

I walk over to her. I have to hide my smile as I realise she barely comes to my hips.

She holds out her hands—two quick, sharp claps.

The wall groans. I take a step back as the white brick rolls down into the ground only to be replaced by a huge, heavy wooden door. The Witch waddles over, reminding me of a baby penguin, and pushes it open with the end of her cane.

Darkness floods the room, and nothing but stark black shadows appear beyond the door. My throat bobs.

'What's in there?' I whisper.

The witch looks up at me, a devious smile playing on her lips.

'Oh nothing,' she waves me off again, adding quietly, 'just my flesh-eating plants.'

'*What!?*'

'Go, little Witchling. I need a pouch of black leaf from my evergreen shrubs,' she says, hooking her arm around the back of my legs before shoving me through the door.

I open my mouth to protest, but the darkness scares my voice away.

A mere ten steps from the door, a bench comes into view, strewn with all sorts of leaves and spices. Some were in pots, some were dried on the table, and all had toothy grins and vicious attitudes.

'The pouch should be in front of my dearest *Camellia sinensis!*' the Witch calls from the entrance. Very loudly.

I sigh through my nose, a sigh echoing beside me.

I glance to my left and see a pouch with a little black leaf painted across the brown fabric. It is beneath a giant plant with a large toothy maw. My muscles freeze. I am going to lose my hand and never be able to make potions again. My fingers twitch slightly in apprehension.

One …

Two …

THREE!

I yank the pouch and tear my arm away, narrowly grazing the leathery mouth of something slimy and sharp. I desperately hope it's the right one as I spin on my heel and hurry out the door.

I've never heard of Camellia sinensis … Why on Earth would she assume I'd know about her hungry Witch-eating plants? I'll be sure to enrol in a herbology class next semester.

I rush through the door, having half an idea to jump completely over the little Witch, but my foot meets the doorway, and I trip past her, sliding on the floor over to the cauldron. The door disappears behind me as I huff, hunched over myself.

'Wonderful,' the witch says, knocking my boot with her cane. Her pale lips adorning a cheeky grin. 'There might be hope for you yet.' She bounds onto the small step stool over the bubbling cauldron.

I stand and follow, scratching my temple.

'Well, go on. Put it in,' she says, picking up a large metal stirrer, and circling the liquid in the pot. I toss the mesh pouch into the boiling water.

The Witch concentrates, putting her whole body into stirring a ladle as tall as she is.

'So, what is this potion exactly?' I ask.

The swirling liquid melts into a deep brown. The Witch's bony elbows are spread wide, and her tongue is poking the corner of her lips. She turns to glance at me, steam covering her pink glasses, and I smile.

'Once a month, the Potion Masters from each coven come here to share their latest recipes,' she says, from behind a curtain of steam.

'Is this your recipe?' I ask, glancing in the pot again. 'Just boiled water, sugar, and herbs?'

'No Witchling, this is what we call tea.'

A strange sound escapes my throat at the realisation.

'Oh.'

She laughs again, making me feel even smaller than her.

'Our recipe sharing is a front,' she starts, 'We don't get to see each other as much as we would like to so, we came up with a way to meet every month without suspicion.'

'Is seeing your friends *that* important you created an entire fake meeting for it?' I ask, dumbfounded.

'Of course, friends are important. Many people come and go, but I'd do anything to keep us connected and growing old together. Surely you have friends like that?' she asks.

I shake my head, my heart clenching a little at the thought.

Friends …

The Witch looks me up and down with a raised brow. 'I find that hard to believe. Friends are easy to come by here.'

'That's easy to say when you already have some,' I bite back. 'I haven't made *one* friend yet.'

'Please, sit,' she says, stirring her finger. Suddenly I'm swooped up by a chair and sitting at a table across from her.

My vision swirls and I grip the table. A tiny ceramic cup with pink flowers painted on it clatters in front of me.

The little witch smiles, 'One or two sugars?'

The Shadow

SYDNEY FRY

*R*eyna managed to hide away, narrowly missing her handmaids and early-to-rise mother. The armchair she'd draped herself over had been shuffled to the arched window to bathe in the morning sunlight. Despite her efforts, the view had been forgotten for the thick book in her lap. It was nestled in the layers of her skirt. Her charcoal-sullied finger traced along the words as she read. She was careful not to mark the parchment with black powder as she had her dress. Reyna batted her mother's scolding from her mind. The woman would have much more to gawp at—the rest of the charcoal was stuffed into her blue bodice.

Blackened parchment lay abandoned beside her, an attempt to alleviate the undue pit in her stomach. Riveting herself with the text did little to ease her either. She closed the volume with a sigh, tipping her head back against the cushion. Dust rose from the pages with a whoosh of air. Reyna watched as it drifted down, filtering through the rays of yellow light. Her gaze fell on the outer grounds. Grey Harbour was full. More commonfolk gathered on the docks than in the courtyard below. She eyed a knight as he boarded the fleet and started from the chair with a gasp. The flotilla—Grey Harbour's small contribution to the war—departed today.

Reyna flew from the library. Her slippers clicked against stone as she ran down the stairs, soft-hued fabrics bunched in her blackened fingertips. Her eyes flitted between the unfolding corridor and the port. At the pace she'd set, she could barely catch a glimpse of it.

Her heartbeat hammered as she wove through the hall. Banners lined the well-lit walls, forming blurs of white and dark blue. The bustle of the outer grounds extended into the castle; the chatter of staff buzzed around her.

Her skirts slipped from her powdery grasp. She glanced down to clutch them once more. In a mere moment, two handmaids appeared before her. Arms full of bedsheets and chattering, her advance was lost on them. With a gasp, Reyna twisted, missing them by inches. Strands of the maid's hair stirred in the rush of air.

Reyna called out her apologies, strained voice echoing off stone as she fled. Her maids shared a knowing look and giggled, watching the whirlwind of a girl hurtle into the stairway. On more than one occasion they'd seen her slip up to the tower accompanied by her shadow. It was the furthest space from the council rooms and chambers, a refuge from overbearing parents and insistent siblings.

Reyna burst from the stairway, hands grasping the stone to stop her momentum. The fleet was already yards free, trailing white lines in their wake. An obscenity escaped her as she choked down air and hunched over. A lump formed in her throat. She had missed him.

Soft clinking drew her attention, turning her head. Her house heraldry, a swan, stared her in the face. Her eyes rose and met his, corners crinkled with amusement. She breathed out a laugh before standing. He bowed his head. Her lungs burned, yet she gave them little relief with short breaths, trying to conceal that she'd torn through the castle grounds. Her cheeks gave her away. So did the beads of sweat across her dark hairline. She bowed her head in return.

'You waited.'

'I did.'

'You aren't going?' She gazed at him expectantly, twisting the thin band on her thumb.

'I am.'

Her eyebrows upturned. 'You missed your ship.'

'There will be another.'

She didn't reply, turning to the bay. She wondered if she would still feel him when he was past the horizon. She always felt him near—posted at her chamber, at the cathedral, with her on this landing. He shifted to stand beside her, his chainmail gently brushing her shoulder.

Reyna's gaze drifted from the bay to the tower wall, tracing his shadow. She turned to him; eyes gleaming.

'Stand still.' His brow furrowed as she dug out a piece of charcoal from her bodice. 'You shouldn't have any trouble with that.'

He rolled his eyes but didn't shift.

Ease fell over them as she traced his shadow. She took her time, despite the rising sun. Once finished, she placed the charcoal on the ledge and resumed her place beside him. They watched the fleet meet the horizon, becoming dark specks on the blue line. He seemed more intent on the commonfolk below preparing for the next departure, yet her eyes barely left his face, committing him to memory.

Their time was cut by the hour bell, radiating up the stone. He took the charcoal from the ledge, knuckles ghosting against hers. He bowed his head, and she in return, glassy-eyed. Reyna faced the harbour once more.

Reyna stood atop the tower, pressed against the stone as refuge from the predawn chill. It had become routine—to evade her handmaidens, slip from her chambers as the guards changed over and return to the landing. Hours would pass before the sun rose and cast orange rays against stone. And still, she waited, drowsy with sleep, for the light to warm her back and cast her shadow beside his. Sometimes, she would raise a hand and ghost her shadow hand down his face.

Most of her time was spent scanning the empty horizon until blue turned to black. Her mind drifted then, though he didn't always occupy her thoughts. Sometimes she dwelled on the developments of the war—victories in the isles and allies in the mountains.

As dusk fell, a maid lit a torch for her. Specks of ash floated on the night breeze. Reyna would tip her head back against the stone to watch as they drifted down, catching it on her palm. Her gaze always returned to his silhouette. The torchlight never stretched far enough, ceding the shadow of her beloved to the darkness that crept at its edges.

Still, she waited.

The Dreaming Drops

Taylor-Anne Collings

*T*he ravaging clash of claws and shadows threaten to swallow me whole if I don't move my damn feet faster. The once familiar beckoning and warmth of my forest home has transformed into one of the many nightmares that have haunted me for weeks. The once familiar pine smells have turned to blood, the soothing, cool breeze replaced. Replaced by those infernal black shadows. My mind is racing; I can't pull a string of rational thought, let alone any spell that'll save my life.

Great.

There is nothing more humbling than having this supposed immense power since birth then not being able to harness it when I need it. If only I listened during lessons to my skilful older sister, Caldweina. Regardless, I muster every spell that crosses my mind. But they're nothing more than pathetic trickster spells. I hurl a Twisted Stepping spell back at the creature, praying to all three Mothers that it changes its course ... no such luck. It is easily swallowed by its copious black clouds. I catch a glimpse of it. It rumbles a few short feet behind me. A mass of swirling, haunting darkness that stares towards me. Long, wispy, tendrils with sharp claws emerge with eerie fluidity, then vanish into its shadows. It smells foul, like rotting flesh and smoke. I whip my head back around in horror, fear tempting my stomach contents to make an appearance.

The brown leaves swirl around my darting feet and dance in the wind behind my embroidered emerald cloak, becoming engulfed by the raging shadow. What I would give to be back in my secret tree hollow instead of this feverish moment from my worst nightmares.

Instead of fighting for my life, I could be tinkering with potions, practising spells, reading my favourite ancient fables, and hearing the contagious laughter of my twin brother.

My heart sinks ... Archie. If anyone can stop this ghastly creature, it's him. He'd be able to destroy it and then earn his right to be an arrogant ass. Although, I suppose he has. His power has always surpassed mine in every way. The famous miracle child: the male born with magic. He's the magical anomaly that shouldn't exist. Of course he was born powerful, and being without him makes me... vulnerable. Not just to this creature, but to everything. It's a shame that I haven't been able to locate him for days. After that ugly fight between Yalkca and Caldweina I walked in on, he just ... disappeared. Shouted vulgar and horrible things at our older siblings that I can't believe he would ever say—then stormed out and vanished.

And he left me behind. He never leaves me behind. We"e supposed to be a team. The aura I can typically sense and follow to find him blocked. Why would he say those things to our family then leave us? Leave me? What the hell even happened to cause such a rift? Maybe I could fix it. But here 1 am, about to be slaughtered by whatever this thing is, with nothing so much as a 'Goodbye'. Tears sting the edges of my eyes, the realisation crashing into me like a heavy blow. I'll never see my family again. Nor hug them. No more braiding Xalkta's hair while we gossip about the coven. Or training my spell casting with Caldweia earning her affection. The most devastating of all, the lost promise of exploring the reaches of the world with Archie.

My body burns from the exertion, my essence fading with each feeble incantation I cast. I can already feel myself fading away. Losing all my essence would be a disaster, even though my spells are rubbish. It's comforting to have something to fight with, anything. A large moss tree nearest to me plummets over encased by shadows, as if foretelling my impending demise. The thunderous crack fills my ears as it rumbles to the floor. I watch as the environment around me transforms into darkness. My rasping breath hitches as a stray root grips my foot, and I fall.

My breath hitches as overwhelming terror dominates my senses. There is no way that the forest has betrayed me like this, it's a mothers-damned outrage. I have lived here my whole life. I thought I knew every rock, tree, root and river. It would seem everything in life hides secrets, even from those who love them.

I fall forever, as if the Mothers themselves are savouring this moment. I hit the mossy, moist floor with a body-quaking thud. Pain reverberates through my bones, leaving me motionless. The icy grip of panic seizing my soul. I desperately will my heavy legs to push themselves up, but I don't move, as if the very spirits of the forest hold me down for deliverance. The shadow pounces, finally catching its prize. It tears into me, burying its frozen claws into my flesh. Once again, the Mothers work their magic.

Despite the cold, it burns. It burns like the furious silver gusts of a winter storm nipping at the edge of my consciousness. The skewering of its claws sears my flesh like it is branding me. My skin is torn to ribbons, blood pouring into the vibrant wildflowers summoning spring. The ice-cold shadow incepts my bones. I glimpse viscera being discarded around us, the nerves in them still screaming. My last lingering thoughts surprisingly aren't of my own mortality—as everyone says nor the excruciating pain bolting through what remains of me, but for my loved ones. My older siblings, my coven, and my twin brother. I must find a way to warm them. I can't just fade away. In a silent prayer, I scream for Archie...

A desperate plea that he escapes in time if he's still here. That he let go of that stupid argument driving him to abandon his family and gets the other two far away from here. That he'll warn someone from the coven, and the coven elders will dispatch this creature and send it straight back to hell. It's all I hope for while I slowly slip away ... Until a familiar aura suddenly ignites my consciousness. The sudden arrival brings the searing and stabbing in full force, trying to coax me into an eternal, blissful slumber. This aura feels ... too familiar. Like home. With all the strength I have left, I slowly slide my eyes open...

Archie.

The Last Snow of Avery

ALISHA FIRNS

I 'It would be better if I died quickly.' Avery sighed, a petulant lilt to his voice as he stared up at the ceiling with a listless gaze.

This was followed by Bells' dispassionate yet gentle admonishment.

'The Duke doesn't like hearing you say such things.'

Both figures were bathed in the gentle glow of the candlelit room, a scene made almost dreamlike by the ribbons of light shining across the silken sheets. Bell gently gazed down at the bedridden Avery, her hand lost in the fluffy white of his hair that he bitterly likened to that of an old crone. As his childhood companion, it was inevitable that she'd remain by his side even in his dwindling moments.

'That isn't my problem, is it?' He yawned, leaning into her touch with feline arrogance.

These exchanges were not uncommon in his father, Duke Edmond's, estate—the grim topics offset by the nonchalance with which it was spoken. It was as if the conversation was that of a minor inconvenience rather than the young Lord Avery's dwindling mortality. His face, a porcelain mask of delicate beauty, never lost its sneer in his sickness. No, such a thing didn't suit the impetuous young lord.

'Your father would likely object to such a thing.' Bell murmured softly, adjusting the blanket to completely cover his lithe form, 'He doesn't wish for his only heir to get sick at such a delicate time.'

Avery had just turned eighteen, the same as her. He was supposed to be at an age where he could travel freely and do as he wished to his heart's content. Being allowed to drink alcohol freely, ride on horseback, dance with a beautiful woman at a ball.

Unfortunately, illness does not bend to these whims.

'My, my, surely you don't believe that I'll actually survive this winter like the rest of those sentimental fools. Surely the Bell I know wouldn't be so silly?' Avery's delicate lips pursed in displeasure, and he turned with a huff to avoid her gaze. 'If you're just going to insist I spend my last days cooped up in this damnable room, then I'll—'

'I understand.' Interrupting him, she spoke without fear and stood from her seat, 'I suppose you wish to play in the snow with me?'

It was a terrible idea, especially with how weak he had been recently. Brashly ordering the window open in winter, enjoying cold sweets and sneaking around the estate without an ounce of care for his health. Avery was a young man who spent his whole life selfishly inviting death at every turn; all for the sake of living.

Bell knew how much Avery hated being cooped up inside, away from the simple joys of life he longed to experience. But his sickness kept him devoid of these simple pleasures, and he hated any who attempted to keep him alive and trapped rather than living his short life in the way he wished for. He felt nothing but contempt for the people who coddled him and did nothing against his tantrums and difficult personality.

'... Well, it seems you haven't lost your senses. I'm glad, Bell.'

His smile was radiant. It was moments like these that Bell understood why she could never deny her most precious person his brash wishes. Stretching across his pale face was a grin so wide it cracked the slight dryness of his pink lips, an expression he rarely offered anyone. Avery was a being who many thought of as a cold and majestic winter, eyes so strong in will to any who could catch his gaze. But to Bell, he would always, first and foremost, be her best friend.

'This surely brings back memories, eh?' He laughed, like twinkling bells, as he built a crude impression of his father from the snow. It was a familiar scene to Bell, his body smaller and gaze more contemptuous in her memories of their first meeting.

'You didn't like me much. You told me to bark since I was a dog bought by your father.' Bell sat beside him. 'I believe I pushed you. And like boulders, we tumbled off the balcony and into the snow.'

'Yes, quite the audacious attitude for a street rat Father picked up.' Despite his sharp words, he didn't look angry. A smile, wide and mischievous, split across his delicate face and Avery looked at her with a fondness reserved for very few in his life. He didn't hate her impudence at all.

Yes, Bell always knew how much he hated being treated so delicately. His pride was always trampled on when the people around him treated him like glass, as if he could shatter at the slightest touch. But in their first meeting, Avery hated her most of all.

In his eyes, Bell was everything he hated about his life. Her body was healthy, and she was brought from poverty to serve as his playmate, to dedicate her life exclusively to caring for the poor, pitiful son of Duke Edmund.

It was why when she stood up for herself, and they toppled from that balcony into a blanketing snow, he felt happy for the first time. It was also the first time he got to play in said snow. And now here, in a time that signalled the end of his short life, they were once more risking his life to play in the snow.

'You know, if I get sick from this and die, Father might order your death as well.' He hummed thoughtfully, but he didn't sound at all apologetic.

'I see. I guess I'll be following you into the afterlife too.' Bell did not sound particularly apologetic herself. She smiled.

And so they played in the snow for the last time; the last snow of Avery.

Soul Uploaded Successfully

ALIES SCHELLINGERHOUT

Click! *You are now awake.*

Mark sat up in his bed. *The sheets feel soft.* The alarm clock stopped buzzing the second he opened his eyes. He swung his legs over the side of his bed, his feet hitting the floor. *The wood feels cold and hard.* Mark looked down at the redwood planks underneath him, the colour deep like fire, capable of eating his toes without warning.

Mark sat outside, a cup of steaming hot coffee in his hands. *The coffee smells rich.* He watched birds fly across the sky with their bright colours, the sun bouncing off their feathers, uncovering a hidden rainbow. The funky, upbeat melody was Mark's favourite song, although hearing it on repeat for days does take the fun out of it.

'Next song,' he muttered, and instantly the birds changed their whistling to a slower, romantic tune all too familiar to him. A hopeful smile crawled across Mark's face hearing the song—it was their song—and now it was only a few hours until he could hold her again. He put the cup against his lips. *The coffee burns. The coffee tastes bitter.*

The bus pulled into the station as soon as Mark walked up. He never had to wait long anymore. The seat looked just like he remembered, though in here it was always brand new. Mark would be the first to 'touch' the fake velvet. The seat was a pristine blue with randomly scattered yellow and red triangles. But the pattern wasn't random because each seat looked exactly the same. *The fabric feels soft. The seat feels firm.*

'Next stop, arrivals centre,' a kind, feminine voice rung out over the speaker. When the bus stopped Mark hopped off, staring at the massive building in front of him. The structure swirled around itself, the wind whistling as it passed the corners creating a beautiful orchestra of sounds. Coloured glass coated the sunlight in different hues, depending on where you stood. It was a breathtaking sight. Still, Mark couldn't help but feel betrayed when looking at it. He was staring at a promise that was nothing more than the most beautiful lie ever created. His feet moved almost against his will, taking him inside the building.

'Excuse me, ma'am. I'm looking for the scheduled arrivals?'

'Of course, dear. Expecting someone, are you?' a tall woman gestured for Mark to follow her. Her heels clacked on the floor as she walked ahead through the large hall.

'Yeah, I've been waiting for a while. Three years, actually,' Mark said sheepishly.

'That must've been hard. I take it you were not expecting to end up here then?' The woman looked at him with kind eyes. She looked happy to be here, but how could anyone be happy in a place like this?

'I was but, I just didn't expect to end up here this early, if I'm honest. Car accident. It was this or death.' *Death would've been better*, Mark thought, but he couldn't say that. The woman looked at him with compassion, the slight wrinkles by her eyes and soft smile curling her lips comforted Mark.

'Well, in my experience those who arrive unexpectedly have a harder time adjusting than those who know they're coming.' The woman took Mark's hand and squeezed it gently. *Her touch feels gentle and warm.* Mark gave the woman a weak smile and nodded. They walked the rest of the way in silence.

'Do you know when she will be arriving?' the woman asked as they entered the scheduled arrivals hall.

'Not sure, just today.'

'Alright, well, there's seats over there. if you want something to eat or drink there is a little café over that way, and they make regular announcements on group arrival times.'

Mark thanked her as they parted ways. He walked over to the window, stretching the length of the wall, unbroken. The golden, tinted glass draped the inside in a warm, comfortable light.

'It shouldn't be possible,' Mark muttered to himself, shaking his head. 'Glass for a wall …' He reached out, touching the window with his fingertips. *The glass feels hard and cold.* He walked towards the café, taking a deep breath. *The smell is fresh and sweet.*

'Next group arriving in 5 minutes,' the same feminine voice from the bus filled the hall. Finally, he would be able to see the love of his life again, hold her in his arms, kiss her. It felt like eternity waiting for the doors to open.

'Mark?' her voice rang out behind him. The same voice that called to him after his accident, telling him everything would be okay. He turned around to face her. She was just as beautiful as he remembered, glowing skin, freckles scattered everywhere and a rosy blush as if she'd been in the sun just barely too long.

'Melody …' She was here, she was finally here. He reached out to touch her face. *Her skin feels soft and warm.* He still couldn't feel her touch. He dragged her into a strong embrace, regardless. *Her body feels warm. Her touch feels firm around your torso. Her hair smells of roses.* Mark closed his eyes, tears spilling down his face. *The tears feel hot on your cheeks.*

'Mark? Why can't I feel your touch?' Melody asked, confused. Mark's heart broke at her words. He looked at her defeated, a painful smile pulling across his face.

The dead don't feel
They merely watch
Living without *smell* or *taste* or *touch*

The living feel
They don't just watch
Living with smell and taste and touch

What happens when lines are blurred
When the dead try to do more than watch
When the dead try to *smell* and *taste* and *touch*

When the dead feel
They don't just watch
Living with *smell* and *taste* and *touch*

Can the dead feel
Can they do more than watch
Can they live with *smell* and *taste* and *touch*?

My Place

KATIE LATTER

*M*y Place smells of sweet earth and honeyed sunshine. Green grass drapes itself over rolling hills and wispy trees sway lazily on a soft breeze. There is a pond here too; in the light of the morning it glitters gold and later, when the night swallows the day, it shimmers a dazzling silver beneath the moon. I can run in My Place, for miles and miles and I don't get tired. I can chase the ducks and the squirrels and the geese forever and I know this is where I am meant to be, for forever.

At least … I did. Lately, the glimmer of the pond has dulled, and the ducks and squirrels aren't nearly as tempting. What is this emptiness? It feels like hunger. Like thirst. Like, no matter what, this hole cannot be filled.

Something has changed today. I can smell it on the wind. It whispers pretty promises that, at first, I cannot decipher and carries a familiar sweetness. Lemons, honey, and the warmth of freshly baked bread.

Her …

Her. Here. In My Place.

That scent alone closes part of that hollowness in my gut and makes my four legs pull me forward. I take off towards the edge of the park, where the steep grassy hills are dotted with tiny white flowers. The grass murmurs in the wind. Coaxing me. Calling me to melt into its softness and roll in the thick, sweetness of daisies and earth.

Not now.

Now I understand that I have been waiting for Her. Waiting to find Her; to bring Her here. There will be time enough for that later.

I run on. My wet nose tilted to the blue sky, clinging to that familiar string of sweetness that hangs in the air, tethering me to her. More flowers burst forth from the grass as I near the crest of the hill. Tulips and poppies and bluebells. A veritable feast of smells and shapes and colours, which expands as I finally find myself at the top.

The Garden unfolds beyond My Place. Birds, flowers and fruit of every colour; a rainbow extending into the sky. A little blue wren lands next to a rose bush with blooms the colour of fresh apricots and a scent just as sweet. Perhaps I will return here to observe the little bird. But it can wait.

I have been here before. My arrival had been sudden. I found myself walking through darkness and then light and then … The Garden. A warmth had spread from my belly to my paws, a warmth and a sense of belonging. A comforting cool breeze had caressed my back and head in greeting and tugged me towards My Place.

As I stand amongst the flowers I feel that same familiar touch in the wind, tugging me towards Her. I hold onto that scent that dances beneath the light curls of honeysuckle and apple blossom; that familiar warmth still blossoming in my chest.

My nose tugs me forward.

Left.

Right.

Right again.

That breeze pawing at me encouragingly.

I start to sprint when I near the end of the rainbow maze and see a bridge made of richly coloured stones. Each one glimmers brightly in the afternoon light like colourful stars. They are cool as rain beneath my feet despite the warmth of the sun stroking their glittering surface.

I sit.

Waiting.

She should be here. This is where I arrived.

I stare at the foreign yet familiar plane beyond. A grey road, lined with bland silvery boxes on wheels. A bicycle tings beyond my sight and some instinct makes my blond tail wag. But do not chase.

I stay.

I sit.

I wait.

The light fades.

Blue sky turns to yellow.

Then to red.

Then to purple.

The plane beyond darkens and little yellow rectangles of rigid light blare through the black night. That comforting breeze is gone. I don't remember when it faded but its absence chills my bones and claws at the returned emptiness in my belly.

She isn't here. She hasn't come.

Such cruelty. Such acrid disappointment.

I rest my nose on my paws and blink back hot, fat tears.

Why was I sent here if not to fetch Her? Had that familiar scent been some trick? Had I dreamed it up? Why isn't she here? I sniff again, no longer trusting that string of smells that had pulled me here. It still hangs on the air, refusing to admit its foulness. Its lie.

The whine that escapes me is wretched. It morphs into a howl that chills the garden and hangs in the now-dark sky.

When I rise, I don't return to my place. Not now that I know what is missing, what the aching pit expanding now with every breath means. I don't follow my nose. I don't listen to the honeyed promises on the now-returned breeze. My body moves of its own, numb accord in no particular direction.

Right.

Left.

Left again.

I lose myself in the maze of darkened, colourless flowers.

Perhaps I will tire, though it is not likely. Perhaps I will collapse and become one with the pretty peonies that sway around me. I cannot help but stare at their petals, still perceivable, even in the dark. Little drops of dew on the delicate pink reflect the stars that now wink down at me, like they know some secret I am not privy to.

Perhaps I will lie down.

The plants in the garden behind me rustle in the wind. I stop.

They rustle again.

I am overwhelmed with the scent of honey and lemons and sourdough. Her!

I whirl around to find a woman emerging from a field of sunflowers that glows gold in the dark. The light dances in her brown eyes and accentuates the silver cascading through those deep brown curls I remember. There are new crinkles on her brow and cheeks and mouth, lines that prove she still smiled, even after I left her.

I stop for a moment.

'Charlie?' she croaks out in a melodious, warm voice.

Charlie.

That was my name.

That's me.

Her eyes don't leave mine as her knees buckle.

My tail starts to move of its own accord; my eyes sting and burn but I don't care. A whimper escapes me.

It's Her.

I am on Her in seconds and we tumble to the soft grass and I am whole again. I pin her down and lick the tip of her nose, unable to get close enough to her. She smiles up at me in the rosy-gold light of dawn that tiptoes into the sky and pets my golden head.

'Am I home, Charlie?'

I bark and lead her back to Our Place. To the smell of sweet earth and honeyed sunshine. To the place where green grass rolls over the earth with its wispy trees and soft breezes. To the pond that glimmers gold in the sunshine and, under the moonlight, shines a dazzling silver.

I lead her here for the beginning of forever.

Sunrises and Sunsets

RILEY HAWKEN

*I*t began not as a competition, but as something two friends had in common. Joel and Sam had been friends since school. They had always enjoyed the outdoors, camping, fishing and hiking. After school, they tread their own paths; Sam studied a trade, while Joel went to university, but they kept in touch. In summer they fished and surfed, in winter they hiked and played golf. Social circles expanded, relationships flourished and inevitably they caught up less.

When Joel and Sam did catch up, they always had a spectacular sunrise or sunset to share, along with a story of how they secured the shot and where they ventured to capture it. Their quest for the perfect sunrise and sunset photograph was bonding at first, slowly becoming competitive. Capturing the better shot became an obsession. They planned date nights, romantic weekends, holidays – every occasion and outing – around shooting the perfect sunrise or sunset.

'See this one at 1770? It's the perfect sunset, Sam! What! You've never been there?

We went last month for Mum's 60th; she wanted to go to her favourite restaurant in Coolum, but I convinced her to go to 1770 and have fish and chips on the jetty so we could… umm… see this sunset. It was so worth it!'

'Worth it for who?' murmured Joel's girlfriend Holly.

'Well, Bec and I have a special anniversary coming up and we are going to Sydney, wait until you see my Harbour Bridge sunset photo!'

'We do? We are?'

'Yeah, babe we've been together two months next month. I was going to surprise you!'

Their friends had been amused at first as they watched the competitive streak of Joel and Sam's relationship play out again. They had seen it many times; on the football field, in the classroom, on the golf course – but even to them this seemed intense.

'Come on guys, it's the same sun!' one of their friends said, echoing everyone's sentiments. Joel and Sam were oblivious, their heads in their phones, showing each other photo after photo of sunrises and sunsets. Each one was undeniably beautiful, but neither could recall the moments surrounding the photos or even the people they were with.

The day Joel had spent on the boat with his father and brother, all too rare these days, was hazy, but he recalled his triumph when he took the sunrise photo.

'Got it!'

'You've got a bite already?'

'Try and beat that one Sam!'

Sam's first date with Bec, a picnic at Mooloolaba, featuring the sun setting over the water, a cheese platter and a bottle of wine; perfection… except for Sam's obsession with capturing the sunset from every angle. Bec sat on the rug alone, thinking how romantic it could have been while Sam ran around snapping photos muttering incoherently about someone called Joel. Well, I've had worse dates… I guess, she thought to herself.

When Joel suggested a weekend at Byron Bay for their third-year anniversary, Holly thought he may propose. When he suggested a morning walk to the lighthouse to watch the sunrise, she felt even more that this might be the moment. As they arrived at the foot of the lighthouse walk, she saw a familiar figure in the darkened distance.

'Hurry Bec! Sunrise is at 5:59!'

Joel looked in Sam's direction. Their eye's locked. They ran, leaving their girlfriends standing alone. They scrambled up the long path, pushing each other out of the way in a bid to be the first to the lighthouse. The sky was painted with pink and orange hues as light broke through the clouds. The sun slowly descended over the lighthouse and the sea beyond it. Holly and Bec stood in silence absorbing the majesty of the lighthouse in the first morning light, ignoring the distant figures of their boyfriends wrestling.

'Breakfast, Bec?'

'Love to.'

They walked off in companionable silence processing what they had just witnessed. As they settled into a café in town and ordered coffee, they both smiled.

'How was that sunrise?' Holly asked.

'So glad we shared it. It was a marvel!'

'You know it happens every day,' laughed Holly.

They chatted over coffee and croissants. Their phones buzzed but they ignored them, still marvelling over the sunrise they had witnessed. A whale breached in the distance to Bec and Holly's delight. Joel and Sam found them as they were finishing their second coffee. The boys approached sheepishly, sat in silence and listened while Bec and Holly chatted. Eventually Bec conceded their presence.

'We saw a whale.'

'Did you get a photo?' Joel and Sam asked in unison, immediately regretting the question. 'Sorry... sorry.'

'Since we are here together let's have some fun! Snorkelling?'

'Awesome I'll just get my underwater camera...' Sam trailed off as he noticed the expression on Bec's face. 'Or ... maybe I won't.'

A Little Reason

BREACH GREGORY

*T*he fire crackles before me, giving off heat which warms the body and lights the tall eucalyptus trees that surround. Usually, this time of year brings warm weather, yet tonight brings a shiver to the spine, a collapse in the wood burning in the fire.

The crunch of dried leaves brings me back. Looking over my shoulder, I smile at Travis walking toward me with a glass bottle of lemon, lime & bitters.

'Thank you,' I say, taking the cup.

He stands beside me, watching our daughter sleeping in my arms, as she twitches against the cold breeze nipping at her red button nose. His eyes shimmer in the campfire light, and I smile at him, gesturing for him to take her.

Unspoken, he squats down and lifts her out of my arms, cooing at her and kissing my forehead on the way up.

I look at the man holding our child, our miracle baby, in his arms and think back to when we first met. It baffles me how someone can one day walk into our lives and change it forever.

'This bloody tyre...' I chucked the lug wrench against the trim with a *clang*.

My abdomen throbbed as if an invisible force had picked up the wrench and started to stab me with it. I fell back and put my head between my knees, savouring the rush of air following a passing truck.

Sweat dripped down the back of my neck and I felt the sunshine begin to burn my skin. My life was falling apart. No, ripping apart. Being quietly diagnosed with the worst Endometriosis isn't exactly sunshine and rainbows.

Taking a deep breath, I looked around, hoping to gather the strength to keep trying. Looking back at the rubber shreds clinging from around the rim, I began to sob. Out of all days, this had to happen on the worst day of my cycle.

'Excuse me, Ma'am, can I be of some assistance?'

I jerked to the side and glanced up to see a man lingering near the boot of my car. He stood still, eyes darting between me and the wheel, his posture tense as if weighing the risk of approaching.

I staggered to my feet; my head throbbed in time with my abdomen. I managed to nod. 'Ah yes, that would be great. I need to change this tyre; the lugs are too tight.'

I watched as he, in two steps, crouched beside the tyre and loosened the lugs with ease. I huffed; in less than a minute, he'd done something I'd been trying to do for half an hour.

'Got yourself a bit of a jam here.'

'You have no id— oh no.' I rushed to my car door, reached through the window for my phone and dialled my gynaecologist. Frantically, I apologised for missing my appointment, deflating further when they explained the next available one wasn't for months.

Clearing his throat behind me, I almost forgot about the man changing my tyre in the heat. Whipping around, I stared at the spare tyre and tools packed away in the boot. Relief washed over me. Now, I could get out of this heat. Guilt overpowered me as I realised the man probably had more important things to do.

'I can't thank you enough. Follow me to the pub, and a beer is on me.'

'Thank you, Ma'am, but there is no need.'

'Please, my name is Maisy.' I reached out my hand.

'Travis.' He took it.

As if a haze had lifted, my vision suddenly cleared, and I began to take in the handsome features of the man standing before me. He was dressed like a farmer, with rugged features and polite manners to match. I cleared my throat, suddenly hyper-aware of the scene I just caused.

'It's the least I could do to say thank you for helping me and putting up with—,' I gestured to myself, '—this.'

'No, thank you, Maisy. Pay it forward when you can; that's all I ask. Where are you headed?'

'Palace Pub,' I lied, realising I had nowhere to be in a hurry.

'Alright, I'll follow behind just to keep the trouble from catching up to you.' He tipped his cattleman hat toward me before returning to his Ute.

Parking in front of Palace Pub, I hopped out of my car and headed for the door. The thought of a cold drink had my body eager to brave the noise which seeped out from under the door. I looked over my shoulder and saw Travis walking toward me.

'You really don't need to walk me to the door.'

'I'm here to see someone,' he said as he opened the door.

'Oh,' I walked through and Travis followed.

'Are you sure you don't want that drink, Travis?'

'A drink would be nice, but that's not how I was raised. I'll buy.'

Not giving me a chance to argue back, he made his way to the bar and grabbed the server's attention. He leaned over the bar and kissed the woman on the cheek, 'Hey Mum. Two lemon, lime and bitters, please.'

I smiled at the gesture and nodded a hello to the woman, before I processed his words. I gawked at Travis as I sat next to him, watching as he removed his hat, sat on the stool, and placed it over the top of his knee. Noticing my reaction, he chuckled.

'You had a few empty bottles rolling around in the boot of your car.'

I smile at the travel cup in my hand and look up at Travis, rocking back and forth with our sleeping baby. Without him, I would have never gotten through Endometriosis treatment. Most of all, I would have never had the support and love to fight the battle to have our child.

Funny, isn't it? How one person can come into a life and completely change its trajectory.

I marvel at it every day.

My Darlings

TAYLA PURVES

*T*he sun rippled through the kitchen, a warm and quiet morning, the soft crashes of strong ocean waves in the distance. How lucky was I to live my island dream? Humming, I made my way around the kitchen island, firing up the stove and getting a filling breakfast started for another day in paradise.

The pastel blue walls were contrasted by the light wooden and white furniture, and dark blue stained-glass vases littered the tops of my kitchen cabinets; Harry hated them, but they were an extension of me and my crazy dreams. Dreams that led us to call Lord Howe Island home.

Breakfast flew by, the coastal breeze whispering through the windows, tugging on each strand of my hair. The sun kissed my skin gently before the heat settled in. Harry had hardly been home for 10 months of the year but today, he'd finally come home to me and my crafty antics. He had been off living his dream as an athlete in Formula One.

He had begged me to come with him, I'd have loved to follow this season, but my painting and the ocean led me here; the soft white sand and crystal blue water a siren calling me like an emergency to be home with nature.

Harry was due for his four-week summer break and although he'd won the race in Belgium just last weekend, he hadn't told me exactly when he'd arrive home.

But I knew it wouldn't be long.

He called me morning and night, pressing me for every new detail on the paints I bought, or the gorgeous dress I'd picked up from the local boutique where I met Annalise, the beautiful brunette who had quickly become like a sister.

My phone chimed from inside, breaking my thoughts of staring at the bright blue sky and the romantic symphonies of the Welcome swallow.

Fitting for Harry to continue our ritual.

I raced indoors, bumping my hip into the island bench, shouldering the hallway corner, and diving onto the grey couch to reach my phone; grinning like a maniac as I answered.

'Hi, honey!' I panted as I answered.

'Hi, sweetheart,' he laughed into the line making my heart soar, picturing his wonderful smile that set the world alight. 'What are you so out of breath for?'

'I was just practising my couch-surfing abilities,' I smiled into the phone, 'I still suck.'

He laughed at my answer.

'What are your summer break plans?' I asked, the anticipation killing me. We hadn't seen each other since March, and it was nearing the beginning of August; I missed him.

'Well, if you open the front door—' he started but I had already hung up.

'Shut up, shut up, shut up, shut up!' I squealed, battling my arms and clunky furniture to the front door; the sun beaming back at me through the windows.

I hurled open the blue front door and there he was. Brown curls a mess, his headphones hung around his neck, his green eyes bright and shining like a prince in armour, my Harry.

'Mi amore,' he sighed, bags shoved to his feet as he leaned forward ready to capture me and my wildness in his arms.

I was in heaven leaning into his hard chest, his chin resting on top of my head and mess of blonde hair.

'I missed you so much.' I inhaled his oaky scent.

'Home,' he whispered into my hair.

I leaned back, my hands making their way to his face on their own accord. His eyes sparkled as they stared back at me.

'You're home,' I smiled.

Harry walked past me into the house, taking everything in, including the new artworks I'd hung at his request. The sun hit them in just the right place to make them sparkle with a kind of casual magic.

'So … what do you think?' I asked him.

His awestruck gaze landed on me, slowly shifting to a smile. 'Feels like home, mi mmore.'

'How about you go and freshen up?' I said, 'I'll put some laundry on and put your bags in the bedroom. I have someone I want you to meet.'

He quirked an eyebrow, but I shooed him. I had hidden an addition to our life. A tiny grey Weimaraner puppy with the most gorgeous eyes. I named her Maple. She was just under twelve weeks old, but she was the light of my life, and the final piece to my puzzle.

I tiptoed my way to her crate in the sitting room, doing my best not to crash into any furniture on my way. I reached down and bundled her grey, floppy body in my arms; her big blue eyes sweetly staring up at me. I got so lost in them that I didn't hear Harry enter the room.

'Who do we have here, baby?' Harry's voice was higher than I'd ever heard before.

'This is Maple.' I let out a little giggle at his squeaky voice. 'She's all ours.' I watched him as he grinned down at her.

'Hi, miss Maple girl,' he cooed as he leaned in and she licked his nose, 'Oh, you sweet girl.'

'You're not mad?' I asked him, the knot in my stomach slowly coming undone. I'd never kept a secret from him. Ever.

'How could I ever be mad?' He kissed the pup's nose softly. 'She's perfect, amore.' He leaned back to act as surprised as she was by the act, and Maple's excited yaps filled the room with a bright, light happiness that warmed my cheeks.

'Maple is so beautiful baby, kind of like her mum … no?'

'I would have said she's gorgeous like you.' I blushed, 'It was so hard keeping her from you.' I pouted at him while he stared at her. She had snuggled in the crook of my elbow and was now slowly drifting to sleep.

'I knew something was up.' His green eyes pierced straight through me, 'Isabella, my soul was trying to bring me home to you. I felt a pull to you even throughout the weekend.'

'Oh, so that's why you were fast all weekend at Spa, huh?' I teased.

His jaw set, and his eyes sparkled playfully.

'You knew I had a secret …' I grinned again, 'Maybe I should get another dog next time I miss you,'

He pulled me back into his arms and we stayed like that, embracing the time together for what felt like eternity.

The Envelope of
Love and Farewell

Nellie Burwin

*E*ngulfed in the darkness of pre-dawn I whispered, 'Georgia, Bobbi, it's time to write our letter to Grandma.' They both sprung out of bed with great big smiles on their faces. They knew our morning ritual: sunrise, surf check, then coffee and babycinos at our local cafe.

When I was five, my family moved from England to Australia. Not my beloved Grandma though. She relocated to a beautiful, French cottage in the countryside of France. The only way for us to connect with her was through letters. Hard to believe it in the 21st century, right? Every month, I'd rally Georgia and Bobbi to write her an update. They were more of a distraction than helpful, but I loved watching them frolic around the beach as the sun's rays danced on the glistering water. Eric, our black and white border collie, would round up the children with his playful antics, making the task a bit easier.

Driving to the beach, the windscreen fogged up and the streetlights illuminated like runway beacons. My heart grew heavy. I remembered how she'd ask about every small detail of our lives, her eyes twinkling with genuine interest. Grandma's relentless curiosity was both endearing and daunting. I could imagine her laughter as she read every update, her ability to recall each tidbit made me feel responsible for delivering every precise detail of news. These letters were a lifeline. Family was so important to Grandma. Every time she would visit us in Australia, she'd orchestrate grand reunions. She was always bringing our extended family together. I strived to uphold and carry the same family values she instilled in us.

The kids' laughed as Eric stuck his head through the headrests like he was stuck in a pillory, giving them slobbery kisses on their ears and cheeks. The wetness left the kids' cheeks glistening and reflecting light like a mirror. Some would say keep the dog's germs away from the kids, Grandma would say let them be, so that's what I do … I let them be and I took solace in their joy.

'Mum, are you okay?' Georgia asked.

'Yes darling, I am fine. Just recapping everything that has happened over the last month.'

Bobbi chimed in, 'I wonder if there will be any swell. We should have brought the boards just in case.'

'Bobbi darling, I need to focus on writing this letter when we get there, we can go out and catch some waves another time,' I responded.

We entered the beach, the air crisp as our bare feet sank into the sand. My big toe cracked through the seamless and smooth surface, like an ice cap. The cold, dark dawn lingered as we waited for the first light to stretch across the sky, painting it in shades of pink and orange.

After I rifled through my bag and pulled out spare kids' clothes with blueberry stains tattooed into them, dog poo bags, drink bottles, snacks, Eric's lead that was once seven metres long but, adorned with knots, is only five, and tissues that could be used for papier-mâché—I finally pull out a piece of paper. Just your typical mum's bag where finding anything is a challenge. After I dug around some more, I finally found the pen Grandma gifted me during her last visit. It felt as though a piece of her was with me as I began to write.

Dear Grandma,

Another letter from your favourite granddaughter and her family. I'm sitting in the same spot as I always do, writing this letter to you, watching the sun rise along the horizon. The warmth from the sun's rays engulfs me like a big warm hug from you. Thanks for that lovely hug. I have been working hard trying to finish off my uni studies. I am nearly there. One thing I will never forget was that you told me how you used to wear the same perfume every day so that the student who was blind knew when you were there. I am going to do that. In fact, I have been doing that since my last placement. Lachie has been great with the kids while I've been on placement.

Sorry, I got carried away … to answer your question, Lachie and I were actually going to ask you whether we could come and stay with you in France, so then I could do some English teaching there. We also thought it would be so lovely for you to see Georgia and Bobbi grow for a little bit. We were thinking of spending three months over there. What do you think? It would be so nice to see you, even better to see you every day.

We love you, Grandma.
Forever and always,
*Olivia, Lachie, Georgia, Bobbi a*nd Eric xx

I placed the letter into an envelope and licked to seal it. Usually, I would fill out the front of the envelope with Grandma's address, but this one was different. I would be entrusting my dad to take it to England. I wrote this letter in the hope she would read it soon. But when I handed it to my dad in the evening, I watched it slip through my fingertips in slow motion as tears welled up in his eyes. I was faced with the saddest truth: Grandma had gone somewhere I couldn't reach and my reply would never find her. Instead, my words would rest beside her as she lay in her eternal, peaceful sleep. I hoped that, by some miracle, she might still read my last letter in her heart.

Though she's gone, I will never forget. I will always carry her legacy with me and hold her love close to my heart. Forever and always, Grandma, we love you. I know this is so cliché, but this is not goodbye—it's a see you soon.

The Green Autumn Leaf

KAIEA MOGNO

*T*he autumn wind whistled through the park, unsheathing a chill that sliced through Mary's coat as she stepped out of the car and into the golden afternoon. The sun threatened to dip behind the tree line, leaving behind a sky bruised with seasonal hues. Leaves crunched beneath her, their colours blending into a honeyed flame that belied the cold. She stood by the car and watched her son gather himself in the passenger seat. He only had eyes for one thing. His fingers fumbled with the handle and managed to crack the door.

'Mum, can we go on the swings? Please!'

'Looks like it's going to rain soon, Jack.' Mary stared at the clouds looming in the distance and back to her son. Jack turned his head slowly, his blue eyes narrowing slightly as his gaze flicked upwards and back to her.

'The swings won't mind, Mum!'

A smile tugged loosely at the corner of Mary's mouth as she considered him. 'No, I suppose they—'

Jack was already clambering out of the car before the words left her mouth. She watched him as he half-ran, half-stumbled towards the playground. The creak of rusted metal snapped the stillness of the damp air as he plopped into the swing seat, the frame dancing in unison with the trees around them. His legs—too long—scuffed against the bark-strewn rubber mat. Mary followed methodically, her steps slow, measured, like she knew every move in this sequence. She had learned this routine by heart and lived it every day.

'Mum, can you make me touch the sky?' Jack's eyes were gleaming with excitement, his voice buoyant. His words flowed with a sing-song cadence; a quality that never left him as he asked a question he had asked her a thousand times before. Mary paused, her hands shackled by the chains of the swing.

'Maybe tomorrow, darling,' she told him gently, laced with a tiredness that grew ever stronger, 'but how about we see how close we can reach?' She started to push, the frame groaning under her son's weight, but she kept going. The screech of metal filled the park in harmony with Jack's growing laughter. It was a familiar sound that once brought her joy, but now it slithered down her chest at a painful pace, coiling deep within her gut. Her arms strained to push him, cold sweat sliding down her brow.

'Mum, push harder!' he demanded with an urgency that struck her.

What was it? She couldn't quite shake the feeling of a mother's guilt, his words dragging up buried feelings. A reminder of the things she could no longer give him.

'You're flying, Jack,' she murmured between laboured breaths.

'Mum, do you wish I could fly?' Jack's expression was serious, his innocent gaze pierced her.

The question stabbed her, sinking into the knot in her gut and uncoiling a pain she could hardly bear. The clanking of chains echoed as her hand unshackled itself from the swing. She blinked, hurriedly regripping it, her knuckles turning white.

'Sometimes, Jack,' she admitted, her voice laden with years of weight.

Jack frowned, trying to process her words and the strange emotion snagged to it. 'Well, we'll keep trying, Mum. I like it when you help me!'

His simple words lodged in her throat and she blinked back tears that threatened to spill. She reached out, brushing a curl from his head.

'Can we get something to eat now?' Jack smiled innocently.

Mary nodded, her hand squeezing his. 'Of course, darling. How about we go to our usual?'

They walked back to the car together, Jack's footsteps noticeably slower as his earlier energy depleted. The sun had since retreated behind the clouds, and the first drops of rain caressed her back gently before escalating into a downpour. Her practised motions guided Jack into the car and buckled him in. She climbed into the driver's seat, gripping the wheel tightly as rain hammered the windshield, obscuring the road ahead.

As they drove away, the sky continued to open and the earth drank deeply, quenching a thirst that had been building for years. Jack's eyes followed the raindrops racing down the passenger window. He had always loved the rain, even as a boy. And now, at thirty-two, he still did. Mary sighed; a sound filled with the weight of decades. She was sixty-two, her hair streaked with grey, her face wrinkled by a lifetime of care. But Jack had remained the same, a fixture of innocence as the world around him changed.

The doctor's words hissed in her mind as the serpent within her gut reared its ugly head.

'He'll need more care as you and Jack get older, Mary. There is excellent disability housing—'

'I'm not placing Jack in a home,' Mary interrupted, her voice sharp.

The doctor simply nodded, his expression one of practised sympathy, 'I understand, but this is for you *and* Jack's sake … For when you can't care for him anymore.'

A week had passed, and the conversation had haunted her every thought, the truth in his words dangling before her eyes. The thought of Jack in a care home terrified her. *How could anyone else care for Jack? Who would understand him like she did?* The future loomed dark and uncertain like the storm raging outside.

'Mum, what's wrong? Why aren't you talking?' Jack's words disrupted her musings.

Mary forced a smile, searching for the right words.

'Just thinking about how much I love you, Jack.'

Jack's face lit up, and Mary felt the world crumble around her as she made her choice in that moment. She pushed it aside and memorised the moment they shared, his smile, and the ease in which she loved him.

As they drove to the restaurant, the rain lessened to a slight patter on the car's roof, a gentle reminder of the world outside and the path that lay ahead. But for now, Mary allowed herself to forget.

Blue Fluff and Unicorns

TIM E. ATFIELD

*L*ily giggled with anticipation as her mother put her in her new pink checkered dress and cowgirl boots. Her parents had been telling her all week about what the Armidale country show had in store for her. Her father took her out of the car and lifted her up on his shoulders, putting his Akubra on her head and telling her to keep it safe for him. Her head couldn't fill the hat and it kept sliding over her eyes.

It was twilight as they walked down the main laneway. As afternoon drifted into night the lights of each stall became brighter. Lily gleamed with wonder as she watched the flashing lights and colours around her. The sounds of slide guitar and mandolins filled the space like they competed to be heard over each fair game stalls' carnival music and the muffled announcements over the loudspeaker. While they walked past the rides, she marvelled at the sheer size of the big wheel going around. As she stood in awe, waiting in line for the Ferris wheel, her mother gave her a stick of blue sticky fluff. All Lily's focus shifted; her eyes widened as she tried the sweet fairy floss. She devoured the whole bag like she hadn't eaten in days. It wasn't until she had

almost finished the treat that she realised they were almost
at the top of the Ferris wheel. She could see the whole show
grounds, making her feel like she was flying. Lily's father
pointed at the oval showing her the monster truck jumping
over a line of half-crushed cars. She couldn't care less; she
kept her focus on the delicious treat in front of her.

As they left the Ferris wheel, the smells of fried food—
Dagwood dogs, doughnuts, funnel cakes and hot chips
cooking in hot oil—wafted through the autumn breeze
as Lily saw all the delicious foods around her. Her father
gave her a dagwood dog, and the family sat down to watch
the rodeo as they ate. The delicious smells of the fried
battered hotdogs soon faded as the cows entered the field.
An unpleasant smell filled the air as the crowd gasped then
laughed as one steer relieved itself. Lily's mother quickly
hurried her away from the area to escape the foul scent,
leaving her father to watch by himself. All Lily could do
was snigger.

As they explored more of the show, Lily was astonished
and excited by all the stuffed toys hanging on the wall
behind a row of turning clown heads. As she stared at the
bright colourful prizes with flashing lights around them,
Lily noticed a little man with a bored, sour look on his face.
He had a vague smile which showed his yellowed teeth,
his eyes looked exhausted and his breath smelled of smoke.
Lily's mother gave the man money as he passed her five
ping pong balls. Lily placed the balls in the clowns mouth,
hoping to win the massive pink unicorn which seemed
twice her size. She was disappointed when all she won
was a stuffed cat the size of her hands. Tears started to fill

BLUE FLUFF AND UNICORNS

her eyes as an old man next to her won the massive pink unicorn. Her mother hugged her tight.

'Aww, don't cry baby, it's what happens with these games.'

The old man approached her and her mother, carrying the oversized unicorn. 'Here! You can have this if you want it!'

'Are you sure?'

'Yeah! I was trying to win the cowboy hat for my grandson anyways, he wouldn't want this.'

Lily's mother thanked the kind old man as he passed Lily the giant pink unicorn, Lily's eyes were filled with joy as she struggled to wrap her arms around it.

As Lily and her mother made their way back to the grandstand, all Lily could hear were the screams and laughter as people rode the rides; they watched the roller coaster as it shook as each cart dropped on the first hill. After they took a ride on a wooden horse on the carousel; Lily's mother lifted her on her hip. The colourful lights shone bright into the night sky as Lily looked up at the towering rides. Then all of a sudden, a sinister laughter filled her ears. There was a dark, scary house with horrid sights all over it. As they walked past the haunted house, a giant scary bat jumped out at them. It had bright red eyes and long sharp fangs. Lily hugged her mother tightly and closed her eyes as they quickly moved away from the area.

'Don't worry Lily, I've got you.'

Lily, with her eyes closed tightly, felt some comfort from her mother's voice as she explained that it wasn't real. 'Just try to think of a name for your unicorn instead.'

As she came up with multiple names for her unicorn, she soon forgot why she was so scared.

Eventually, they met with her father. He had been watching all the events going on in the oval and had a playful smirk on his face.

'Oh my! That's a big unicorn!'

Lily giggled as he took her off her mother's shoulders and hugged her. Suddenly, there was a loud bang in the sky, and then another. Voices everywhere started to gasp as the dark sky was lit with bright scattering colours. Lily and her parents watched the fireworks above the show grounds. The loud pops and bangs scared her, but she knew she was safe in her father's arms.

As Lily was carried back to the car she drowsily gazed at the glimmering carnival lights over her father's shoulder before drifting into a slumber.

The Weight of Reflection

Kelsi Davis

I bumpily drive up the side of the curb and perform a parallel park my parents would be ashamed of. I take a deep, shaky breath and admire the surroundings, as if for the first time. The street is lined with bright green lawns, and double storey houses with large windows and big, wooden front doors. Huge trees loom over the perfectly smooth road—but there is not a fallen leaf in sight. I slide open the visor mirror and try to wipe the dry streaks of mascara off my cheeks. My eyes are red and puffy, and my skin is blotchy.

What's the point? I think as I open the car door.

After two knocks, the bright red front door is slowly opened, revealing a small, middle-aged woman. Her head hangs out through the half-open door, and uncertainty washes over her face before she realises who I am.

'Ellie!' she yells enthusiastically, suddenly the door is wide open and her arms are around me. She pushes herself off me but keeps hold of my shoulders. 'Aww … what's wrong, baby?'

And just like that, I'm undone. I start to sob, and she brings me into another hug, this time not letting me go.

There's something about a mother's hug that draws out all the feelings you've been burying.

'Aww, darling, what's happened?'

I take a deep breath to avoid a shaky voice. 'Is Dad home? Can I come in?'

'No, El, he's away until Tuesday for work. Come in, I'll make some tea.'

Sitting at the countertop island, I watch Mum flick the kettle as my legs dangle off the stool like a helpless child in a booster seat. Mum grabs the jar of tea leaves from the pantry with one hand and grabs two teapots from the cupboard with the other. She places it on the counter that divides us and begins to spoon dry leaves into the ceramic pots.

'Your father was just asking about you the other day,' she says. 'Just checking up on you.'

'Mum,' I dismiss. I haven't spoken to him since last Christmas, and even then, he showed more love and compassion to the flies on the pavlova. 'Jacob proposed.'

She looks up at me, her green eyes glazed with confusion.

'I didn't know what to say,' I continue.

She manages an apologetic smile. 'Oh, El.' She rushes around and wraps her arms around me again. I embrace her shortly, then pull away. Shame riddles up my spine and I suddenly feel very small. Mum plops herself on the stool beside me.

'Cold feet, love?'

'No. I don't think so,' I respond. I pick at the loose skin on my fingernails. 'I um …' I peel a piece of skin and feel it sting. I watch as the blood slowly leaks out. 'I've been seeing Dad in myself.'

I look up to meet her eyes, and her brows are furrowed. 'What do you mean, El?'

'It was perfect, Mum. Jacob is perfect. He's done everything right. You know that. You've seen it when we visit. He's always so kind, and he puts everyone above himself. He's perfect, Mum.' I look down to my hands again. 'But I've started to be mean … like Dad.'

I tell her how I would get so angry at nothing and take it out on him. How I would find ways to project my insecurities onto him without meaning to. How I would treat him like a dog, ignoring him whenever he did something I didn't like. And how, like a dog with a bird in its mouth, he would wait for me to take notice of him. Exactly how my father treated me when I was younger.

Her eyes are wide, and her lips part with surprise. 'Oh, El,' is all she could manage.

'I don't know why he proposed, Mum. I've been so cruel.' I look back down at my hands, unable to look at her. Suddenly, they hurt unbearably. I tore more skin while confessing, and my fingers are as raw as I feel.

'I remember when you were little,' she starts softly, 'you would raise orphaned joeys, and birds with broken wings. You would chase butterflies for hours and give every ladybug a name. You've always been kind, Ellie. And I know you're not that small girl anymore, but I think that she's still in there.'

Through distorted, blurry vision, I return my gaze to her. There are tears in her eyes that weren't there before.

'Honey, I love your father, and I know he and I have had our ups and downs. Just like you and your father, even though you don't get along anymore. But I also know that you're not him. You have a heart that's so good and pure he couldn't comprehend it. He may have given you your blue eyes, but there's warmth in yours, where only coldness lies in his. And he may have given you your name, but that's where your similarities stop. You're not your father, Ellie. You're the furthest thing from it.'

She stands up and embraces me again, and I crumble into her shoulder. Sobs shake out of me, but Mum doesn't let go.

'Now, I know this isn't what you want to hear, but you need to talk to Jacob. Tell him how you're feeling, El. Or how you're confused, at least. I'll be here waiting when you need me.'

I hug her tighter and breathe out a hot sigh. 'Okay, Mum,' I reply. 'Thank you.'

'Anytime, sweetheart.'

The Wedding Guests

JESSICA CLOW

*T*he duck was inside the unit when Mackenzie walked through the front door. It was small and brown, with vibrant orange feet and green streaks on its wings. Unfurling itself from beneath her coffee table, the duck ruffled its feathers and quacked impatiently.

'Is that duck still in your unit?' Leah's voice crackled through the phone.

Mackenzie groaned. 'Yep.'

'Girl, you need to get rid of it.'

'Trust me, I've tried, but it just—oh my God, can you leave me alone for two seconds?'

The duck had waddled across the living room to meet her, brushing its feathers against her ankles like a cat.

Another quack. *No*, she imagined it was saying.

'Call your landlord or something,' Leah said.

'The bloody thing always disappears when he comes around. I swear he thinks I'm hallucinating.'

Mackenzie dropped her bag in the hallway with a thud and kicked her thongs towards the shoe rack. Leah began talking as Mackenzie changed the phone to her other ear, but she only caught Leah saying, '—start a duck removal service.'

'I am the least qualified person for that.'

The duck quacked again, its bill reaching up towards Mackenzie. Its black, beady eyes bore into her, void of emotion. As she walked down the hallway the thing trailed behind her, babbling like a toddler.

Mackenzie slipped into her bedroom and shut the door. The duck's shadow waved across the carpet as it paced on the other side, its quacks muffled through the wood.

She pressed a hand to her ear. 'Sorry, what was that?'

'How'd it go with your folks?' Leah asked. 'Are they coming?'

'No.' Mackenzie sighed. 'Mum was adamant. I don't even know why I bothered trying, to be honest.'

'I'm so sorry, Mack.'

'It's fine,' Mackenzie said. 'I'm just sorry *you* have to deal with this.'

'It's not your fault your parents won't accept you.'

'I know.' Mackenzie breathed in slowly as her eyes began to water. Tear stains from the drive home were still glued to her cheeks, and she vowed not to start crying again. She was stronger than this. She was above this. She was going to have a better day because of it.

'I love you,' Leah said.

'I love you, too.'

'Do you want me to come over?'

'Is it alright if I come to you?'

'Of course, babe. Whatever you want.'

Leah's breath carried down the line, soft and comforting. Mackenzie focused on the sound and let her own breathing mirror the soothing rhythm. She wasn't alone. No matter what, Leah would be there.

Maybe that could be enough.

Mackenzie's hands fidgeted with the white ruffles of her dress, the lace rough against her fingertips. Sunrays streamed through the window and danced across the desk, illuminating the bouquet of lavender beside the mirror. She closed her eyes and inhaled, allowing the sweet scent to calm her.

The door creaked behind her, and she opened one eye.

Allie waltzed into the room. 'Everyone's here,' she said, stopping behind Mackenzie and resting her hands on the back of the chair.

The two of them looked at each other in the mirror.

When Mackenzie didn't reply, Allie raised an eyebrow. 'That was code for "Are you ready?" and generally, a question requires an answer.'

'Do you need to be so cryptic?'

Allie just shrugged. 'Let's go. Leah is, I'm sure, waiting *very* impatiently.'

Mackenzie followed Allie out the door and around the back of the house. The sun was warm on her face, bright and inviting.

Allie squinted down the garden and lifted a hand to her forehead, her nose scrunched in confusion. 'Do ducks usually live so far from a water source?'

'What?'

Mackenzie followed Allie's gaze across the garden. A line of ducks marched around the side of the house. Some with orange feet, some with pale brown, some with a green or purple streak and some without. There must have been dozens waddling down along the grass in a long line— towards the wedding setup. Mackenzie and Allie found themselves following, eyes fixed on the curious sight.

The ducks continued towards the chairs and down the aisle as though they were simply late guests. Their colourful feathered streaks glistened in the sun like crystals. Leah, waiting in a beautiful white suit, was the first to spot them. Her hands flew to her mouth as she laughed, the sound ringing across the garden.

Leah's mum jumped from her chair and whipped out her phone. She pushed others aside to let the wedding photographer through, who knelt in the aisle with the camera shutter clicking.

One by one the ducks hopped onto chairs, squeezing three or four to a seat. They settled comfortably and ruffled their feathers, as though bobbing on water.

But the duck leading the pack pushed its way back through the stream, past the seating, and up the garden towards where Mackenzie and Allie stood. The one with orange feet and a green streak.

It stared up at Mackenzie, black eyes bright in the sun.

Leah was looking at them when Mackenzie glanced up. Her eyes crinkled as she grinned and blew Mackenzie a kiss.

Mackenzie wasn't sure petting wild ducks was a safe thing to do. But she figured if one is your housemate, maybe those rules don't apply.

She knelt, the hem of her dress in the dirt, and ran her finger along the duck's head as though it were merely her cat. The duck bowed its head with her movement, quacked once, then trotted off to secure a spot for the ceremony.

Allie laughed. 'Okay Mack, what *on earth* is happening?'

Mackenzie and Leah got married in front of a full house. Their kiss was celebrated with applause and an explosive round of quacking.

Blinded By Love

Holly Dodd

I remember the dark, stormy clouds rolling in, the heavy downpour hammering into my windscreen, the screeching blades working overtime. I remember the song playing on the radio … The details of that night will haunt me forever.

'Isabelle … the injuries you sustained during the accident are extensive. When the other car T-boned you the glass window shattered with such force some of the pieces got lodged behind your eye, damaging the nerves. We're unsure at this time if you'll be able to see again.' The doctor's voice drifted further away with each word. I couldn't care less about my hip being broken, the surgeries could fix that, and the bruises would heal eventually. But what would I do if I couldn't ever see again? I was blind and basically crippled.

They say that those who lose their sight fixate on their last memory. For most people it's the last time they saw their family. Of course, my brain had to focus on the worst day of my life. A vivid memory on loop like a broken record. Over, and over, and over. Wet road. Blinding lights. Then an endless pitch-black abyss.

Many surgeries later I was on the road to recovery, though it didn't feel like it. The doctors were constantly in my room, checking my vital signs, physical therapy, was I drinking enough, how was my fluid output, what was my pain level. It was never ending. I felt as if there were too many people and yet no one. Once I was strong enough to get myself into a wheelchair to use the bathroom, I would sneak out to escape the never-ending number of robotic doctors and their dragged-out processes. My favourite was to visit the courtyard, which is where I met the one person who treated me like a person and not just a patient: Alexander Johnson.

The first time we met I remember feeling like I wasn't alone anymore. I kept going back to the courtyard just to talk to him. Sometimes he would talk about anything and everything, other days when I was feeling alone and down, he would describe to me sceneries.

'I'll always tell you how the world looks, so you always remember the little details,' he assured me.

Months later, my last hip surgery was completed and I was slowly building tolerance for walking again when the doctors came to me with a plan to restore my sight. In the 16-hour surgery they would remove the broken glass from behind my eyes, followed by laser therapy to promote healing of the nerves. Alex decided I should face my fears before the surgery.

So, there we were one morning in mid-August, staring at the small car—well, he was, I was just believing him that there was a car there.

'No. No way I'm getting in. I won't.' I never wanted to get anywhere near a car again. But Alex was adamant that everything would be fine.

'Isabelle … do you trust me?' he whispered.

'You? Yes. The car? Absolutely not.' I truly did trust Alex.

'Then trust me, you'll be fine.' When I finally sat inside I didn't feel safe, but I trusted Alex. I knew he wouldn't let anything bad happen.

I came out of the room still in pain after my eye surgery, I was truly on the road to recovery. I could walk properly again, I wasn't as terrified of cars anymore, and my eyesight would be back again. I couldn't have been more ecstatic.

I couldn't wait to see Alex. I had wondered what he looked like—did he have brown or blond hair? Did his eyes match the sky or the trees? Once my vision was back, I snuck out to the courtyard as soon as I could. Deep brown hair and golden eyes. This was him; this was my Alex. I walked closer, my face hurting from the smile on my face. Slowly he looked up, but he wasn't smiling. Why wasn't he happy?

'Alex? What's wrong? Why do you look so … down?'

He stiffened. 'Isabelle, there's something I need to tell you.' *Oh god, is he leaving me? Maybe he doesn't want me anymore?*

'Iz … the person who crashed into you that night—' I stiffened, '… I was the other driver.'

No. Oh god, no. He moved towards me. 'I'm sorry.'

I stepped back, causing him to stop. *No, this can't be happening.*

'I trusted you. I let you see the vulnerable parts of myself, I let you in. I got in a car with you!' Everything was supposed to be ok, I was healed, I could see again, I was supposed to have my Alex ... 'Did you make me fall in love with you to ease your guilty conscience? Was any of it even real?' I yelled at him. *How could he have done this to me?*

'Of course, it was all real to me.'

I didn't believe him, I wanted to, but nothing was the same now. *How could I ever trust him again?*

'I don't even know who you are anymore, Alex. I'm sorry ... I can't ... I can't keep loving you knowing you're the reason for all this.'

Alex looked at me, his eyes teary and broken—now he knew how I felt—and then walked away. I watched him leave, my trust and heart crumbling with each step.

Everything was supposed to be ok ...

What's the Point

HEATHER GIRARD

*a*s a child, I wasn't too focused on what I was supposed to do as an adult, because those years seemed so far out of reach. I am now in my 20s, and some say I still have my whole life ahead of me, but I've already lived through so many things. So ... where do I go from here?

Growing up, I was constantly doing extracurricular sports: gymnastics, ballet, running, softball, soccer and swimming. I was actually a swimming champion all throughout school—maybe not always the best, but good enough to place top of my age bracket almost every year. I even went to State a few times, which was pretty cool ... and terrifying. There's something about standing in an Olympic stadium, surrounded by teenagers who have trained to power through the 50 metres like their lives depended on it that made me feel ... inferior.

Despite the amount of sport I did, I never broke a bone. Well, I did fracture both of my ankles—which I think technically counts as breaking, so I take back what I said before. I fractured the left one twice playing soccer, its ligament will never heal properly so now I walk a little funny and sometimes it gives out altogether. But I've gotten pretty good at catching myself on the way down.

I found out recently that I have minor scoliosis and hypermobility, which explains why I'm so injury-prone; it only took years of going to the doctors over and over again to get the diagnosis. Living with chronic pain has actually made my ankle issue seem so small. Almost every day I wake up feeling like something in my body is wrong.

But most doctors I go to say, 'Oh, you're so young, you can't possibly have nerve damage. Have you tried drinking more water and exercising? Here, go on the pill and blah, blah, blah.'

Sir, I have had shooting pain on the left side of my body for almost a week and I can't double knot my shoelaces without risking being unable to untie them. I'm pretty sure that's what nerve damage is.

So, I've learned to manage my pain myself and I've found that painkillers help … sometimes. Other times the pain gets so bad I gulp down a packet of Panadol and half a bottle of melatonin in order to sleep through the night. I'll admit it may not be the healthiest option—and I am exaggerating slightly—but it's the only thing I've found that works.

When I was a kid, much like other kids, I witnessed many different forms of love. I saw my parents love each other in their own ways, then another way on TV, and then something else entirely.

My parents would tell me, 'Oh honey, love is different for everyone. You will understand when you're older.'

So, when I thought I had finally found love, I thought it was just … different. Looking back, I don't think it was love at all. I don't think I am actually suited for the kind of love people expect.

I learned recently that I tend to idealise relationships in my head and ignore the signs in front of me. For example: I hate texting and small talk, I really don't like sharing my personal space with other people and as soon as they get too serious, or too clingy, I want out. At the time, I felt awful about it. I thought I'd ruined something that could have blossomed into an amazing connection with someone … but that beautiful connection was all in my head. In reality, he was clingy, obsessed and ignorant. He treated me as if I wasn't a real person, just some object used to satisfy his needs.

Sometimes I don't feel like a real person.

I don't feel things the way other people do—or the way people say I'm supposed to. I feel isolated, trapped in my own little bubble of apathy and some days it seems like there's no way out of my head.

And it's as though the universe is out to get me, constantly throwing awful things my way. Sure, I have gotten through it, but it still weighs me down. There are days when I lay in bed wondering: *Why should I bother? Why should I keep going? What's the point?*

That's the answer though … there is no point. I have learned that life itself has no meaning. We as a species were not put here for any specific reason, so why shouldn't I spend my meaningless life on this tiny blue speck trying to enjoy every minute of it?

I did try ending it all once. I just didn't feel like I could fit in anywhere. I was so stuck within myself I couldn't think of any other way to go on. I didn't go through with it, obviously, but that is a part of who I am, and I refuse to ignore it, as depressing as it may be.

I could go on to say, *I'm not that person anymore!* But in reality, I am. I have grown and matured, sure, but that little girl is still inside of me, deep down, watching us continue to live. It's all for her. Everything I do is for her. No one should have given up on her, and I will not start now.

I have lived through so many things and I am happy to say that *I have lived.* I know that my life has been a mess—that I am a mess—but I also know that I am human. I am me. And as I sit out on my balcony, basking in the luscious golden hour, surrounded by people who care deeply for me, I know that wherever life takes me from here, whatever the universe chooses to throw at me, I know I will be okay. I will live.

Arachnophobia

Aneesa Machin

*T*here's a spider in my bedroom.

It built a web in the corner of my window.

I noticed it as I was heading to bed. It was slightly smaller than a five-cent coin, but that was enough to spark up my nerves like sheet lightning.

> 2am. And alone.
> Who the hell could I call
> in the miniscule hours of the day
> just to shoo a bug away?
> Who would come for me?

Nobody would come for me.
And if they did?

The teasing, the snide remarks—unprovoked mocking and passive aggression.
I once said, 'I wish I could go camping.'

'How are *you* gonna go camping? You can't even sleep in your house without calling for help.'

Like I don't know.
Like it doesn't endlessly taunt me.

I had to deal with the spider myself—
but I couldn't.
I couldn't do anything.
I couldn't kill it.
I couldn't ignore it.
I couldn't catch it in a glass to let it outside.
I couldn't do anything.

I sat on my bed
          —staring through the darkness—
at the small dot in the corner of my bedroom window.
I stared at it for hours; neither one of us moved.
After a while, the world around me melted away …

And the spider was the only thing I could see in this void with me.

The cacophony of car doors and coughing engines yanked me back into my bedroom.

The window had turned from black to amber.

my body—
from my Shoulders
to my Pelvis—
ached from sitting static
on a mattress for countless hours.

The spider hadn't moved either.

Keeping my eyes locked on the spider, I laid myself down and cradled my knees up to my breasts. I fell asleep instantly.

It was still there when I woke up.

It's still there two months later. It's almost doubled in size since that night.

There's something else in the web.

I creep closer and see the translucent body of another spider curled up beside her. An exoskeleton that has been sucked dry.

A male.

I'd been calling her Donnie. Now I think I'll call her Lilith.

I wonder if she'll have babies.

I never thought I'd be ok with a spider in my bedroom.

But it's kind of nice not to be the only living thing in the house anymore.

I can't keep plants or pets because—hell, I can barely keep myself alive.

But the spider keeps herself alive; plus, she's out of the way.

Even *I* can't fuck that up.

After that first night, I tried so hard to get rid of her. I thought about smushing her or spraying her or catching and releasing her. I even grabbed the vacuum; I thought I could suck her up without getting too close.

Any time I'd get near her—thinking I could break through the electrified fence of my nerves—I'd freeze …

I was stuck in a liminal space

Let her live and   Kill her and
I live in fear   I live in guilt
    Fear sizzles the sinews, but Guilt is excruciating, too.
           The pain of guilt or the pain of fear—
                        which is lesser?
                   How do you choose?

I couldn't choose.
So, I chose to do nothing.
Does that mean I chose fear?
Or does my fear of guilt eclipse fear itself?

        I never chose to be afraid of spiders.
            I never chose to be afraid of *everything*.

        I don't think anyone chooses to be afraid of anything. Fear is an awful feeling. Fear is terrifying. Fear, hunger and lust—reminders that we are just animals, that we are just mortal. Maybe that's why we try to get rid of those feelings as soon as we have them…

They're why I dread going to bed.

There are nights I lie awake in a damp sweat, heart pounding, nerves on fire as my mind reels with thoughts of bombs blasting, stomachs groaning, gilded burgers, and my own powerlessness. These nights are as ghastly as those where I lie awake in a damp sweat, heart pounding, nerves on fire as my mind surges with thoughts of deep moaning, hips grinding, tongues sliding, and a cock writhing between my thighs.

On either night the space beside me feels infinite.

But I'm not alone anymore …

I haven't seen Lilith in a few days.

I've checked around the house, looked in all the nooks and crannies, but I can't find her.

I had a nightmare the other night that someone came into my house and sprayed her with poison. She was twitching and thrashing in agony for so long.

And all I could do
was watch her suffer,
powerless to help her.

I woke up with my face sticky and buried in the damp pillow.

She disappeared the next day.
I'd hoped she'd left a plague of wriggling babies behind—but the web is empty.

I got a goldfish today. I named her Chloé.
She flits and floats among the plants and rocks
While I change my sheets and scrub my plates.
It's nice to feel another life here with me again.

After I'd numbed to the searing fear, Lilith became a part of my room. Something about that small dot in the corner of my bedroom window revealed a part of myself hidden in the liminal space.

A strength in the void.

Wherever she is, whatever she's doing,
I hope she's happy …

The Last Smoke

J.A. SCHILLER

*I*ntermittent headlights blurred past while I stood under glaring fluorescent lights. A gust of air swept towards me, picking up the thick smell of petrol and burnt rubber. My head throbbed. I placed the cigarette between my lips while the hose pulsed. It was the only thing that could keep me awake. Resisting the urge to close my eyes, I tore my hand out of my jacket pocket and flicked open the lid of the brass lighter.

'Hey!' The wide-eyed assistant flailed her arms with her vest flapping around her like yellow wings. 'You can't do that!'

My brows drew together. She whirled around and hurried inside the service station screaming and waving to her colleague. My thumb dragged over the spark wheel.

'Hit stop! Shut it down!'

It seemed to happen in slow motion. My eyes drifted towards the flame sparking to life. The unlit smoke fell from my mouth. At that moment, the chorus of Johnny Cash's 'Ring of Fire' echoed around me like a bad joke. Smoke seemed to sit still above our heads, like a veil looming over us while mournful music came muffled through the haze. The singer, the man in the dark corner, releasing intermittent wails, and the stupefied woman, slumped over her table, weren't what held my attention. It was the fact I'd been sitting there for what felt like an eternity.

'You gonna get out of here?'

I dragged my eyes away from the glass between my fingers and looked at the bartender. He was leaning against the counter behind him, polishing a glass with his cloth.

'What?'

'Are you getting out of here?'

'To go where?' I scoffed. 'Is this purgatory or something?'

A mystic smile reached his lips and he shrugged. 'Not quite. Think of it as a transit station.'

My face twisted. 'How do I get out?'

'You have to find the way yourself.'

'What happens if I don't leave?'

His eyes darted to the wailer behind me then lowered to the glass in his hand. I looked over my shoulder and grimaced. The wailer, with tear tracks over pale cheeks, was staring into space. He looked lost and hollow as if a part of him died ... again. I could feel a similar hollowness beginning to open—no, it'd always been there. It just grew deeper. I had to leave, but I had nothing.

I was a forty-year-old man. I rented a small house in a not-so-great suburb. I worked, got home, ate dinner, and watched TV. I had little family and no close friends. My entire existence was hollow. Even how I died had no meaning, just fatigued stupidity.

I felt suffocated like the haze, the smoke, the veil over us, was entering my lungs and threatening to choke me. I tugged at my jacket, and a weight in my pocket hit me. I stilled. My stomach churned while I reached my hand in. The scuffed and scratched metal felt familiar beneath my fingers. They wrapped around it as they had done many times before. It stung—burned—yet I couldn't let go. I sat it on the bar and sneered. The lighter glinted under the bar lights as though it had its own halo. This was a joke.

I received it from my aunty when I turned eighteen. It was an odd gift to give, but she was odd. Aunty Denise was someone whose mind was always on the run. She could be fun; she could be exhausting. But she was good.

My childhood home was barely a home. It was dark, dim and devoid of light, aside from the bulb flickering by the front door, forever waiting for someone to come. When she was around, the lights were on and music would thrum through the walls. Pots and pans would be thrown about with food strewn over the benches. The barely used stove would be alight and the scent of homecooked food warmed the cold house.

Sitting at the table at fifteen, I poked at the thrown-together plate of sausages and mash.

'They love you, you know?' she sighed and slid into her seat.

'Do they?'

'Of course!' Her confident smile was blinding.

I pursed my lips. 'Then why aren't they ever here?'

'They work so much so you can live a good life.'

My teeth ground together. A harsh clang rang out as my fork clattered onto the plate. 'But they're never here!'

There was stilted silence. Her brows were pulled together, eyes lowered and lips pursed. She tapped her old brass lighter on the table. Guilt enveloped me. I ruined it.

'I know they're not here—'

'But you are.'

Her frown melted into a smile. 'I always will be, Danny-boy. Happy Birthday!'

I went to bed that night listening to Aunty Denise tearing them apart. Warmth gathered around me. I slept better than any other night.

I looked at the lighter. I hadn't thought about her in a long time. She passed from lung cancer—of all things—but she went with that same old smile on her face. My fingers brushed over the metal with a softness I forgot I was capable of.

The scuffs no longer looked dirty. The scratches no longer a sign of fatigue. Instead, it looked as though it had its own life. It wasn't cursed. It lost what I lost. It saw everything I did and more. It was a companion who was gifted to me, not to remind me of only the bad, but the good too.

As I brought it into my palm, warmth swam up my arm and filled in the gaping hole … just like one of her hugs. A culmination of memories, grief, happiness, loneliness all gathered and merged.

I looked up at the bartender who stood in front of me with a smile.

'Goodbye, Daniel.'

Morning Brew

Megan Maddocks

*E*very morning, Alice opened the doors to her coffee shop with a smile. The lingering scent of ground coffee and fresh pastry like a warm embrace. As the day went on and the city woke up, a well-loved melody of clinking coffee cups and chatter played aloud.

Every morning Alice greeted the same man, grey haired with a face full of lines that told stories of a life of laughter and warm smiles. Nothing in Alice's life was as sure as this man's presence at her coffee shop. When that bell sung out at 8:30 in the morning, she knew who she would find at her counter. No day was complete without his presence.

'Your usual?' He would give a polite smile, subtly telling her to wait, while he perused the same selection of baked goods behind the glass cabinet. He would browse his options for a few minutes, the queue behind him growing impatient for their all-important caffeine fix. Alice didn't ever rush the man.

Every morning the man would order the exact same combination. Alice found amusement in his routine.

Waiting for a day he chose something other than a medium long black and a fresh maple pecan danish.

Today was no different. At 8.30am, the bell above the door did its dance. The man entered, but something was different. The sunken shoulders and absent expression were out of place in a room so full of life.

Alice didn't know much about him. She didn't even know his name. However, she knew his coffee order and that was all she really needed.

Alice's barista was staring at her in disbelief as she rushed through each order of the remaining customers with barely a smile. Until it was the old man standing in front of her.

'Good morning, how are you?' She beamed at the man. But rather than responding, the man simply gave her a nod and proceeded to order.

'A medium long black and maple pecan danish. Please,' the man said with a smile that looked more like a pained grimace. Alice just stared at the man in surprise as he failed to browse her pastries for the first time ever. He mumbled his order without a second thought.

The man stood looking as though his body was in the room, but his mind was elsewhere.

'Your total is $12.50, sir.' Alice spoke softly when the man made no move to pay, scared to spook him. He snapped back into himself with a nod, taking his wallet out and fumbling around for the cash. The coffee shop seemed to silence itself as if it was purposefully making it more awkward.

'I'll bring it over shortly,' Alice said after the man paid. She watched as he shuffled over to his usual spot, a dark cloud seemingly following close behind. Alice may not know this man, but now she was determined to.

'Here you go, my friend. Your usual medium long black and maple pecan danish.' Alice set down the man's order in front of him. But there was no reaction. The man just continued to stare out of the window, looking at nothing in particular.

'You must be a fan of my pastries, hey?' Again, the man didn't respond. Alice wasn't the type of person to intrude or pry into people's lives, but lately she was learning that was not necessarily a good quality. Sometimes people need a little push to open up, some persuasion to get something off their chest. Otherwise, they tend to suffer in silence.

'You know, all these years of you keeping me in business, I've never gotten your name. I'd say that's criminal, knowing your coffee order and not your name.' Alice sat across from him. He turned to look at her slowly, a bone deep exhaustion weighing down his features.

'Harry-' the man sighed, 'my name is Harry. Very nice to meet you, Alice.' Met with a confused look, Harry simply nodded at her name badge. Of course.

'I really don't mean to pry, Harry, and feel free to tell me to leave you alone, but I couldn't help noticing you might be in need of an ear,' Alice said.

There was nothing for a few seconds as Harry stared at Alice. She could see the dilemma on his face, the back and forth. He kept opening his mouth as if to talk before closing it again. Finally, he spoke.

'It's been three years today since my wife died. Sally was her name.' He paused and Alice couldn't find the words to say as the reasoning behind his gloom was revealed. 'Maple pecans were her favourite; she never did order anything else. No matter how long she would spend checking out her options, it was always a maple pecan.

'She would have absolutely adored yours,' Harry said, looking back at Alice with a wishful smile. 'Our morning coffee together was my favourite part of the day. I started coming here not long after she left me. I couldn't quite bear sitting alone drinking my coffee without her next to me and when I saw the maple pecans, well I took it as a sign. 'The great coffee doesn't hurt either,' Harry continued with a chuckle.

Alice was lost for words. This shop was her life, her pride and joy. It was also tireless work that sometimes she took for granted. She had never considered that something as simple as a pastry and coffee could be such an everyday wonder in someone's life.

Alice couldn't stop from reaching across the table for Harry's hand. He gave a soft understanding smile at the tears in her eyes. She didn't have to explain. He knew what she was feeling.

'There will always be a coffee and a pastry here for you, Harry. And if you have time, I'd be delighted to hear more about your beautiful Sally,' Alice said. The look in his eyes suggested he would like sharing those stories.

Barista's Guide to Composure

Mara Neuendorff

A persistent beeping pulls me from the deepness of sleep. I scramble out of bed to turn it off before the noise wakes everyone else. It echoes. I swear I turned down the volume last night. In the quiet, my heart calms as the winter chill nestles into my bones. A deep breath as my brain maps out the plan for today, settling into the rehearsed routine.

As I eat lukewarm vegemite toast and stare at blacked out windows, the tension in my shoulders does not subside. I wish it were the cold, but wrapped in two jumpers I cannot trick myself into believing Queensland temperatures would drop that far. The weather app says it's eleven degrees outside. Eleven isn't bad. It was eight last week.

My toast is now cold and clumpy as I chew. The last of it goes down with a forceful swallow and a single gulp of water, but no more lest I need the toilet in the middle of the breakfast rush.

Five-fifteen, I search for my keys on the entry table. There is barely enough light to see, but the green of my key chain stands out just enough. A faint 'bye' from Mum. I woke her again. I ease the screen door closed and I'm free to walk to the car without waking anyone else. A wind blows through me. A deep breath to remind my body to stop shivering. It only makes me more tense. Nobody wants to be tense on a Sunday morning.

Ten minutes later, I nose into a parking spot. I reverse and drive in again. Car off, time check, five-nineteen. Good, I have a moment. Breathe, you've handled Sunday alone before, breathe, you can do this.

With great reluctance, I pull my bag over my shoulder and push open the door. The wind, oh so joyful, swirls around me, kissing my cheeks and nose. It cools yet leaves the heat of anxiety, so I walk with my head down and hood up.

In the glow of the café lights, the transformation begins. My hood goes down. I take my hands out of my pockets and flex my fingers against the cold. Rolling my neck and shoulders, I neutralise my expression. Finally, I put a little pep into my walk, cross the threshold of the shop and leave the rest of my personhood outside. I am a barista. I tuck my bag into a nook, poking my head round the corner. Chef is hunched over some pastries. We greet each other. Out front, I wash my hands and let my brain settle into the comfort of work mode as I go about opening.

When the first person walks in, the performance truly begins. My smile pulls tight on my cheeks and my voice is high and fake, I barely recognise it. Double shot oat cap. A churchgoer, a Sunday school teacher, I think. She's nice, soft-spoken.

The morning regulars filter through slowly. Two half-strength lattes. Iced long black, cap with sugar and two caramel lattes, one lactose free, both extra hot. Large flat white. Vanilla latte and banana bread. In the laziness of the morning, I revel in the sounds of milk steaming, the smell of coffee, the satisfaction of a perfect pour. A sweet little heart atop the drink.

The calm does not last. By seven, there's three tables and more people waiting for takeaways. Chef is working on meals out back. I have an overwhelming number of orders, each with multiple coffees, and two fresh-pressed juices on top of that. A man in a tank top looks impatient. He's always angry, always complaining. I look down and my hands are shaking. The milk heats up in what feels like slow motion. I'm wasting time.

He stares at me. His frown pinches further down. I force my shoulders to drop, neutralise my expression into a sweet smile and feed false joy into my eyes. I'm enjoying myself. Take a breath. Next step, what's the next step?

Shots, milk, pour, run. Simple as that. I plate up two lattes and run them with quick small steps. Smile as I place the drinks down. This is fine. I enjoy this job. I am calm. Quick step back to the counter and repeat.

Time passes. I don't know how long, but the rush slows. There's time to breathe now. There's time to get water. There's time to clear tables.

With an arm full of dishes, I spot her walking up the path. My shoulders drop and my smile doesn't hurt my cheeks. It happens every day around this time; sun high in the sky, Mrs Laurel comes in with her wheely-walker and colourful hat to order a small cappuccino and lecture me about the need for more gluten-free options.

Sure enough, she walks up to the table I'm clearing, with a simple 'hello' as she places down her bags.

'Hello, fancy seeing you here.'

She laughs and there are few sounds sweeter than an old woman's laugh. 'Well, this is the best café around.'

'Oh, yes.' I walk inside the café with her, 'The staff are particularly fantastic.'

She blinks at me, confused. I flip my hair performatively. She gives me a sympathetic smile.

'Just your usual today? We've got the carrot cake back.' I swing round the counter and tap her order into the till.

'Yes, that sounds delightful. I'm so glad Chef made that again. It is very nice. You know, this is the only café around here to have so many gluten-free options.'

Laurel pays and I begin to make her coffee. Listening to her monologue, I nod along, comment where needed, putting all the love I can into her coffee. Weighing out shots. Steaming milk to perfection. Realising suddenly today doesn't seem that bad anymore. Pouring a perfect little heart and covering it with chocolate powder. It's the least I can do.

Beans of Time

RYLEY HALING

*I*nside a buzzing coffee shop, a young historian sought shelter from the bustle of the city. As she prepared to order, a book jutting from the bookshelf caught her eye. *Beans of Time.* Blowing the dust off the cover, she opened to the first chapter.

Ethiopia – 845

'Kalid! Here boy,' the young boy called into the dense Ethiopian scrub. Rami was a young goat farmer—14 years old, but already in charge of a small pack of his father's goats.

'Kalid!' Rami was getting frustrated. As Rami approached a small clearing, Kalid darted out from the scrub, bouncing around energetically. Examining the bush with a new-found curiosity, he plucked one of the berries. Biting into it, he felt a surge of energy course through his body. Wide eyed, he ran back towards the village.

A child ran past, distracting the historian's train of thought. She sighed and turned the page.

Makka – 1445

Omar was awoken by the smell of kaffa. Ever since the traders first shipped the strange beans over to Makka from the forests of Ethiopia, the people of Makka began experimenting with the roasting process. Downstairs, Omar's mother was roasting some kaffa in a thin, circular metal pan—a method they had mastered. Upon roasting it, they crushed it in a mortar and pestle, then, combining it with hot water, they made it into a drink. Omar would deliver the kaffa in large pots to the local qahveh khaneh.

The historian quickly put the term into Google. *Qahveh khaneh—a Persian term for coffeehouse.* 'Right,' she muttered as she scanned the room. She turned back to the next chapter.

Naples – 1653

Matteo was woken by the loud clanging of bells. Jumping out of his bunk, Matteo raced down the granite stairs into the courtyard. A small crow was perched on the red terracotta roof tiles, its eyes on the prize. A small horse-drawn cart clattered along the cobblestone road, pulling to a halt in front of Matteo's courtyard.

'Mr Romano, how are you today?' A small, rotund man hopped off the cart, the contact between his shoes and the cobble announcing his presence to the whole street.

'Ah, Lorenzo, good to see you my friend.' Matteo shook his hand, a warm smile across his face.

'I've got the finest beans in all of Naples, imported fresh from Ethiopia, just for you my man.'

'*Thanks again, Lorenzo. I'll have your olives ready by the end of the week.*' *Matteo placed the crate down and waved as Lorenzo departed.*

Walking back to his door, Matteo smiled at the crow on his rooftop. He threw him a few beans, to which the crow responded with—

Her reading was interrupted by a scuffle between two birds outside, fighting over half a croissant. She chuckled and turned to the next chapter.

Massachusetts – 1773

John took a deep breath, then relaxed himself. It was now or never. Protestors from multiple colonies had gathered at Boston Harbour, where three British ships had docked, fully loaded with tea. John and his gang from the Sons of Liberty movement had donned Native American costumes and were convening behind the tavern near the docks. Sneaking onto the ships was the easy part—the British were fast asleep after the voyage. Dumping the crates was not going to be so easy. After three hours, they had successfully dumped 342 crates into the Boston Harbour.

'Let's head back to the tavern, hey fellas?' John led his gang back to the tavern as the sun began to rise. 'Hey bartender, I'll have a beer thanks,' John called as he opened the door, smirking to his gang.

'Sorry sir, we can only serve tea or coffee,' the bartender responded, pointing at the clock.

'Well, that's a shame. Guess I'll have to have a coffee then,' John chuckled, glancing out at the remaining tea crates floating in the harbour.

A man tapped the woman's shoulder.

'Excuse me, miss, are you going to order something? We have paying customers who want a seat.'

'Just one more chapter, then I'll order something.' The man nodded and walked back behind the counter. The woman flipped to one of the last chapters.

Brazil – 1884

'Hey!' A voice sounded from the edge of the plantation. Rafael looked up, spotting a small, volatile looking man.

'Back to work, you're wasting precious time!' Mr Garcia was furious. He'd lost four slaves that week, all from heat stroke and starvation. Rafael was one of only seven left on the plantation, and one of the weakest. At seventeen, Rafael was also the youngest on the plantation.

He held the carefully woven straw basket in one hand, picking the coffee beans with the other. Mr Garcia had implemented a daily quota of ten baskets, and Rafael had only reached three, with the sun setting quickly. Without thinking, Rafael put some of the beans in his mouth and swallowed them. After nothing happened, he sighed and kept picking. Then it hit him. A massive boost of energy flowed through him, and before he realised it, he had filled eight more baskets.

'Meu Deus, that's better boy!' Mr Garcia yelled out, a rare smile appearing. 'C'mon now, its supper time.'

A grin spread across Rafael's face.

Melbourne – 2024

Chloe smiled. 'What a great book,' she muttered.

'Can I help you, mam?' the youthful looking barista called from behind the counter.

Chloe, snapping her trance, realised she was standing at the counter, staring at the menu.

'Sorry, I'll just grab a uh … medium cap on oat milk, with two sugars, thanks.'

'That'll be five fifty.' The barista took her change and returned to the coffee machine. The grinder whirred, spitting ground coffee into the portafilter, which was then placed under the machine to produce the smooth, but rich espresso. Chloe's gaze shifted to the milk jug being steamed, the oat milk circling in the jug like a whirlpool.

'There you are.' The barista handed Chloe her coffee. 'Have a great day,' he said. She smiled.

Coin-versations

WILLIAM MABB

*S*hit, that hurt being dropped. Where am I?

'Hey mate, I'm from Australia, where are you from?'

A rough looking fella said, 'не, мен қазақша сөйлеймін.'

Wonder what that means. So many others to talk to, anyway, thought Chumpy. Beautiful place here.

There were so many people of all races and ages, some walking very fast and others taking their time. Some were running around like headless chooks, while others seemed stiff as a board. Some were eating vast amounts of fried rice, while others were polishing off unfathomable amounts of Carlsberg.

Chumpy felt like he was lost in space but maybe some others could explain where he was and where he was going. He was heading on a lads trip with Jacob.

An announcement on the loudspeaker suddenly blasted, 'Last call for flight number 3K686, LX177. Jetstar Asia, Swiss Airlines, leaving gate B9.'

Well, I guess that's it, no way I am making that flight on time. I will miss Jacob. I had been with him since 2001. Always there, barring those few times I got lost. Every time had been the time of his life.

Well, that busted-up mate wasn't helpful, maybe someone else will be.

Chumpy inquired what looked to be a holey looking one.

'Hey, do you speak English? Where are we?'

The holey-looking girl took some time to respond.

'なに が したいですか、 日本語 と 韓国一ご だけ お話して ください'

Confused, Chumpy tried to say sorry, but realised it was probably futile to apologise in a language they wouldn't understand. Surely the next mate would be helpful, maybe the one with the snake in his mouth. *He looks a bit different, maybe I shouldn't talk to him.* But so did everyone here and everyone seemed to be getting along—just the everyday marvel of international airports.

Why are you donating to the charity box? Save it for a 50-cent cone. Do these people ever stop tossing around?

Feeling pretty nervous, Chumpy mustered up the courage and spoke to the guy with a snake in his mouth.

'Hey mate, I'm from Australia. Do you speak English? I'm a bit lost here.'

Snake-mouth paused for a moment and that got Chumpy feeling like a cat on a hot tin roof. Surprisingly, Pozole responded … and even better in English.

'Hello amigo, my name is Pozole,' spoken in a vibrant manner.

Chumpy breathed a sigh of relief to finally find someone that could speak his native tongue.

'But I speak little English. You're better off speaking to the American but he's very cocky.' Pozole laughed like a hyena when pronouncing the word cocky.

'Well, see you around, amigo, and enjoy your snake,' Chumpy said, feeling a lot more confident than before. It had been a roller coaster of emotions for young Chumpy, a little topsy turvy but it seemed like he was heading to the paradise city.

Chumpy heard someone showing off about how many places he had been—*must be the American.* Not wasting another second, Chumpy finally asked the American, 'Hey, it's Chumpy, what's your name and where are we?'

'My name is Tater, nice to meet y'all. We are in heaven, that's where we are, cowboy,' he said in the most southern accent, with slowed and elongated vowels.

Chumpy thought about this for a second. *Does that mean … Did I die? I didn't know we could die.* Chumpy felt like he was spiralling and probably looked like a stunned mullet.

Tater finally broke the silence. 'I mean that in a good way. Look around you … How many beautiful girls are here and just over there are some Europeans, they're pretty mint looking don't you reckon?' The southern accent was even thicker now so poor Chumpy couldn't understand certain parts of what Tater was saying.

'Well, that does sound awesome. Any advice on where I should begin?' Chumpy asked. *I have never formally been with anyone but maybe it's time I try.* Chumpy felt nervous about trying to talk to ladies, making him realise how rusty he must be.

But then seeing the most beautiful, round-shaped thing in the world, he had to try and speak to her. Her head glistened in the overhead light, capturing her every angle ... Admittedly only three angles and she did seem very shallow at that, but her head was big—just like Chumpy's—and that was enough.

It seems impractical for me to speak to her, but I suppose it seems impractical for me to say anything at all.

'Name is Chump Change, but everyone calls me Chumpy. Do you wanna buck?' Instantly regretting the line as soon as it came out, Chumpy felt as if he had been caught with his pants down. Literally anything else would have been better.

But to his surprise ...

Penny snorted.

'Haha, that's original. I am happy to buck but only if you want to pound, too?'

'I can't believe you said that. I have waited my whole life for someone to say something so romantic.'

Chumpy couldn't believe it and before he could think of something equally romantic to say, the words came out. 'I love you. Your humour is so original. You are the one. Marry me—it would make so much cents if you do.'

'I will. Nothing makes more cents than to spend the rest of my days in the Kuala Lumpur airport charity box,' Penny said.

'Oh, so that's where I am. But that doesn't matter. It doesn't matter who carries us, doesn't matter where we end up—I found love and that's worth more than all the coins in the world.'

Well, aren't airports everyday marvellous things?

The Shiny Bear

COREY FREIND

The mushrooms lay dormant on the tent floor. Left in the safe confines of a zip lock bag. The right side of the tent wall pushed inwards as the protruding nose of the bear sniffed closer and closer. The bear stopped for a second and then with a quick motion of the left claw, a new entrance was slashed. Deranged by hunger, the bear quickly ate the mushrooms, bag and all. A strange taste invaded the bear's tastebuds, it wondered if eating the mushrooms was a bad idea, but as it went to sit down on the ground it felt the earth give way as the Alsakan forest swirled around it. To the bewilderment of the bear, solids had become liquid, up was hiding, and to the bear's horror, branches grew out of each of its shoulders. The small bear inside the big bear's brain expressed fear through the clacking of its mouth and postured itself to its hind legs. The bigger bear followed suit and stood up on its hind legs as well, staring at its new shoulder extenders. Two different birds perched themselves on either side of the bear's shoulders. One bird was black as the night, while the other was strangely coloured with a red face, black tipped wings and the rest white.

The bear had to focus back in onto the forest and the world around it. Two paws made land as the bear got up to its hind legs and stared down into the forest. The forest seemed to stretch out indefinitely. The bear stares, trying to connect shapes to each other... was it a tree... was it a predator?

'Now you see the world for what it is, can you feel the pulse of life?'

The bear looked over to the black bird, its beak wide open. The red-faced bird then began to talk. *'Ignore that half-wit, it only wants to lure you into a mirage, you need to find something and kill... feel that thrill of life by taking it.'*

Conflicted between two voices, the bear felt its mouth... it was dry. It took the familiar path to river, it was reminded how when it was a young cub, its late mother had shown him to be careful not to look around and go off from the track. The path opened to reveal the water that flowed down the river, the bear went over to the riverbank and stood there for what felt like seconds... or maybe hours. He watched bugs crawl about in the mud and dirt. Occasionally, a bug would look up to acknowledge the titan above them.

'Do you wonder what you would be like if you were their size?' The black bird stared at the bear, searching for an answer that it would never receive. The bear wondered how these bugs go about their lives... do they fight over territories? Do they protect their cubs? Do they dread the changing of seasons in fear of hibernation? Do they fear death?

'That does not matter, what matters is that we are the bigger size... the dominant ones, a ruler to subject power over

them… Lift your paw up and demonstrate your power.' The bear followed the red bird's orders and lifted his right paw all the way up till it couldn't move, the shadow loomed over the bugs.

'Why would you want to take these lives… What actions constitutes this treatment?'

The bear felt all the bugs looking at him. Silently waiting for their sentencing. The face of destruction glared down upon them, the red bird stared in anticipation and glee at the coming carnage; few creatures could resist that corrupting pull. The paw slammed down into the muddy ground, squishing a few bugs and scattering the survivors all over the riverbank. The unlucky ones fell right into the river and drowned. The black bird watched with mournful sorrow as the branch it perched on had begun to rot from the inside.

'You smell that… that fear… They will forever be changed by this action… relish in that fact.' The bear took in that bashful pride as he left back onto the path, forgetting what he originally had come here to do. The path started to move, twisting and turning but the bear didn't care… he had gotten used to the tricks the forest was throwing at him. He was now on a war path, paranoia replaced by pride… that feeling of euphoria. The black bird had tried to speak as he trudged down the track; its protest fell on uncaring ears. The bear hadn't even noticed the rotten branch and with it the black bird had left. But what he did notice was… something… different… something… beautiful. A shiny bear rested just off the dirt road; the bear was enraptured with it.

'Go on take it… take what is yours to have!'

With the red bird's blessings, the bear ran to the shiny bear and skipped formalities to start the mating rituals. That feeling of power, dominance and raw emotion overcame the bear, it was something that he had never experienced… it was something that never wanted to let to go… it was great… he was… he… it had forgotten. The red bird had disappeared, so had the branches. The bear opened its eyes to see its paws rested on a strange metal object and its sacred parts were awfully close. In both fear and confusion, the bear ran deep into the woods while three men had been watching from afar.

'Dude… that bear just totally fucked your car.'

The Trees Have Eyes

ALYSSA O'SULLIVAN

*I*t began on a day, not unlike this one. The sun was shining, birdsong rang out through the grove. And the trees … Oh, the trees … They sang their own kind of song. The wind made their leaves quiver in the gusts. It was enchanting and inviting. I was there. The grove was alive with these remarkable trees. With us. The clones, as we are referred to.

You may be wondering why they call us clones. We are all one singular living organism. Our root system connects us beneath the ground. It's deeper than that though, we are exact genetic replicas of each other. But you're not interested in the trees—the foundation of this ecosystem— you probably want to hear about what happened to the human on that day. The one with the strange contraptions.

He came along as the sun was setting. We were getting ready to sing. The whispers spread of someone new in the grove. We were all curious to see how long he'd stay. He set up a triangle of cameras around the centre cluster of clones.

The grove is large and there are many of us here. It is lovely to have such a large family. I find it soothing that even in such a vast area, it can be so peaceful. We don't get

163

many visitors, so there is excitement when someone comes by. I wonder if more will come after you …

You feel familiar to me. Perhaps you should go … You came to this place unprepared.

Can you hear it? The beginning of the sweet whispers that will turn into an alluring melody. We sing beautifully, don't we?

Are you trying to fight it?

You really should go. Now.

Like you, the human, who was as much a part of me then as I am part of the clones now, was waiting for the singing to start. The singing began when the moon was at its peak in the starry night sky. I remember the thrill and excitement. The grove was dappled in moon and starlight. It was a glorious sight.

The human's machines buzzed as he hopped between them. The raucous noise buzzed for hours. The others didn't like it very much and they grew louder and louder, but the human didn't seem to understand the warning. He became more animated and erratic, flailing his limbs about. What is the point of such tiny branches? They seem pointless. Humans are always poking trees, prodding, ripping, tearing. There is so much violence towards trees when all we strive for is to create and nurture life.

Look at this peaceful paradise. We create the perfect habitats to accommodate sweet little creatures for nesting and hibernating. The animals give back to us, they help us help them. Unlike the humans with their noisy machines that cut and tear and mulch us into bits. They take and take, always wanting more.

I'm glad to be rid of my destructive limbs ... at least I think I am ... They did have other uses ... to hold ... connect with others ... to touch. But that's all in the past. I don't need that anymore.

I don't need weird human limbs now that I am connected to the clones. They surround me, keep me safe and warm. They welcomed me as one of them.

We could share our wisdom with you. We are linked; one big root system that shares everything. I can't remember what it's like to feel disconnected—as you are—to lack the certainty that we have. You would like it, I think. The certainty that you'll never be alone, that you'll always be understood, that you'll be kept safe. We can guarantee that. Once you become one of us, there is nothing we would not do to protect you. You will never need anything again.

Do you want to know what became of that pesky human? I continued making a racket with my sophisticated machines. At first, I was only scanning the trees, but then I started taking. At first, it was just some dead branches and leaves. It was when I decided to take a living specimen, I sealed my fate.

I reached for the youngest among us—the one that was not yet fully integrated into our roots. I thought I was being careful, uprooting the sapling completely. I didn't understand it would sever the connection. The young one would not survive without the family. I paid the price that others paid before me. The one you will pay.

Just as now, the fruits began to grow.

You shouldn't have taken one. Perhaps that was my fault. Did we tempt you with the smell of honey and citrus?

As a human, I ate quite a few. They're intoxicating, aren't they? That sour, lemony burst followed by the soothing sweetness—it's divine. I still remember the way the honey coated my tongue as I gorged myself on them. I hadn't noticed the roots sprouting at my feet. I hadn't noticed anything until the first root snaked its way up my body and plunged itself into my eye. I was, of course, paralysed by that point. A scream, from the shock of it, stopped in my throat as it coiled carefully around the back of my eye socket, severing and replacing my optic nerve. I felt it branch and smaller limbs wriggle deeper into my brain. I don't think I've felt anything like it before. They have finally stopped, and I never will again.

Can you feel it now? Can you feel the warm embrace of clone minds reaching towards you, welcoming you in? Can you feel the root system weaving into your inner thoughts? It's connecting you.

Soon all you will feel is our love and protection.

Unhinged

TAYLAH SMITH

*T*housands of tiny cockroaches crawled up her back, and chills shot through her body. Crushing fear gripped her body, locking her in place. Her throat burned from the rawness of her unending screams. She was begging, praying for someone to hear her, for someone to help. Metallic blood filled her mouth, making her gag at the bitterness. Her face contorted in pain as her tongue slopped along the cut on her lip.

Hayley took a deep breath, mustering her strength for another desperate plea for help.

It has been eight months since their horrific murders; 243 days since she last heard her parents' voices or hugged her little brother. 243 days of non-stop interrogations from police as they tried to find out what happened. 243 days of agony at the loss she endured. Not a night has gone by without waking, screaming at the images of their lifeless bodies lying on the floor, their blood pooling around them. Hayley thought the only pain she would endure for the rest of her life was the loss of her family. Yet here she was.

'PLEASE, CAN ANYONE HEAR ME? Please,' she sobbed, 'pleas—'

'Don't bother, dear. We are far from anyone willing to help a little girl like you,' a cold voice interrupted.

The man began to chuckle at the fear enveloping Hayley's face. She felt her pulse quicken, pounding like a frantic drumbeat of fear and despair. Hayley's skin paled at the deep, raspy voice. She forgot all about the blood dripping from her cut and swollen lip; forgot all about her aching throat. She tugged her wrists forward, the restraints biting into her skin, cutting off circulation.

Recognition pierced her, sharp and sudden. She'd heard this voice before. She'd listened to this sadistic chuckle as he saw the fear overwhelming his victims. He was back. And this time, he would kill her.

'Remember me?' he crooned.

Hayley stared at the silhouette of the shadowy figure before her. She knew without a doubt in her mind; this man killed her family. The man who had tried, and failed, to kill her. Her eyes darted frantically through the shadows, searching for any glimpse of the killer's face.

Her throat constricted, the image of her parents faces contorted in terror, the frantic cries of her brother. The smell of burnt wood hung heavy in the air, dragging her back into the ruins of her home, a suffocating reminder of the flames, the screams, and the bloodshed that consumed her life eight months ago. Her body trembled, torn between rage and fear.

'What is it you want from me?' she spat out.

She could see the shadowy head tilt, assessing her every move.

The man finally spoke. 'Your father got exactly what he deserved. His mistake? Going against me. And your family's death? That was his punishment.'

'Look, I don't know what he did, but please let me go. I won't tell anyone you took me. I'll say I got lost walking around. Fell down some stairs or something. Please ...' she begged desperately.

The shadowy figure grumbled in annoyance before taking a step forward. Hayley recoiled at the grotesque sight of the man before her. Her lips curled, and her nose scrunched in disgust as she stared at the large, gruesome scar tangled like a vine across his face. It was puckered and red, extending to where his white eye stared into her flesh.

The light gleamed off the large knife in his hand; blood still caked along its edges. His low, husky laugh echoed in the room.

'Sorry about that. Lucy over there was more fun to play with than I anticipated. Didn't have time to clean up.' His head tilted towards the corner of the room as his eyes gleamed at the memory.

She felt bile creep up her throat, burning her chest. Hailey tentatively turned to face what he had pointed out. Her hair stood up. Every inch of her skin broke out into goosebumps. Somebody was in there with her. Somebody had been there the entire time. Somebody, who was dead.

A loud gasp left her mouth at the decaying figure perched in the corner. Her body lying in an unnatural position; dried blood covered her slender figure from where it had oozed from the various cuts left over her entire body.

Her attention snapped back to the vile man before her as he took a menacing step forward. He grinned down at her, his white eye gleaming with excitement as he raised his knife. She opened her mouth to beg for mercy but was swiftly cut off as his knife plummeted down, slicing through her leg. Agony laced her voice as her ear-piercing scream rang out through the damp room—blood spurt from her thigh, soaking her clothes.

The man looked down with hungry eyes at the knife glistening with fresh blood.

He leaned forward, his knife grazing her temple.

'Oh, I'm going to enjoy this,' he mumbled eagerly.

The man turned around, waltzing over to a table Hayley hadn't noticed before.

'Let's see. What do I want to use next? What will hurt the most?' he snickered.

He turned around with a large butcher's knife. Slowly creeping towards her.

'HELP. SOMEONE, PLEASE HELP ME! SOMEBODY!' she cried out in terror, pushing her body up against the wall to escape the vile being.

He lurched forward with the knife. She heard the snap as the large knife severed her bone and met the cold concrete floor. Pain shot through her body, and light danced around her eyes. She wanted to beg, to scream for help. She wanted to run away. A choked sob escaped her lips, but she quickly stifled it; her determination hardened like a steel bar in her gut.

She imagined her family and friends as the darkness finally took over, and she slumped to the floor. Losing consciences and at the mercy of the unimaginable horrors to come.

Salutations

ASHTON HAWKINS

*D*arkness crept in early, swallowing the fields in shadow before the clock even hit five. It was then a curt *BLIP* sounded across the field, causing my head to turn. Even in the dusk and with crops vying for my vision, I could see the white screen of my computer flicker from the house - a tiny beacon amid the black expanse. My weathered features, normally weighed down by a stony jaw, were almost immediately conquered by a smile.

'Huh,' I said aloud. It was silly to think about, but I had found myself audibly surprised when the expression snuck onto my face. Then again, up until recently, a smile was typically a rare tug upon my cheeks. With every notification—every question or quaint greeting—that tug became that much less of a stranger. Getting a pen-pal was, I thought at the time, the best decision I could have made. Living off the land with no family was admittedly a lonely venture, and aside from one-sided conversations with the livestock, a dialogue was as scarce as a holiday. So, a friendship was a welcome development. While I only messaged during the late hours of the night—typically after a hard day's work—I was not about to pass up this chance.

I stood up from the arable beneath my feet, dusting myself off and expecting a nice spring breeze to softly tussle my hair. Instead, I captured the land in an eerie painting; an unnatural stillness grasped everything in sight, right down to the wispiest stems of grain that surrounded me. No wind. It was not a moment after that I noted just how alien the sky was. It was as if I was viewing it from under the ocean's surface; a great shadow blanketed everything, leaving no room for the moon's light to leave a lustre upon anything. Instead, the moon's radiance was absent, and no craters littered its surface, leaving it as a pale blind eye scouring the terrain. The stars were just as strange, with their light seeming to sift down into muted pillars that dotted the land. This strange aurora captured my eyes and, for the first time in a long while, left me in wonder. I turned on my heels twice over just taking it all in. It was only when I whipped back to look towards my home that I noticed something off. One of the beams ahead of me, once still, began to swing gently in my direction. It was almost elegant, like a spotlight tracking a dancer. It was almost… observing. Call it instinct, but my legs instinctively buckled, and I dropped face-first into the coarse dirt to evade whatever the ray might have been. I clung to the earth, my hands like vices so as to not betray my shaking arms. The light quickly rolled on and passed me by. In the second it lingered over me, I could not help but gasp when it seemed to grab my legs and pull upward fiercely. As the beam swiftly fled, my body crashed back into the field with a hoarse 'oof'. I stifled a groan as I rolled onto my back, watching the light retreat. The pillar zigzagged across the plain, each movement delayed between sudden stops and starts. Such erraticity reminded me only of an anxious, searching gaze. I turned back to face towards the house and summoned up the courage to continue onward. A friend counted on me, after all.

Thus started a nightmare—what I can only describe as an hour of wading in mud, within a forest of crops under a canopy of eyes. The ghostly lookouts had me stopping every meter of stinking soil my elbows kneaded, my shaken breath pooling saliva at my arms. Sometimes, the lights would pass right over me, and my ribs would continue to get bruised from each violent pull. When I finally reached the veranda of my home, I shakily rose to my knees. I made quite an entrance for myself, producing a slimy red carpet leading from the stairs where I wobbled all the way to the base of the door. It was only after I heaved up the contents of my stomach that I noticed something. The entire time I had been in this mess, my heartbeat drummed in my head. When the blood finally drained from my ears, the silence immediately took centre stage. I had to dare myself just to peek around the railing of my porch, because I knew what I would see when I scanned the pens: nothing. Not a single animal hollered or bleated (as if I could see them in this gloom). I squinted, only then noticing the torn roofs upon the coops, gutted like fishes and stripped of their meat. I scrambled inside at the registration, barring the door behind me. Darting upstairs and into my room, I grabbed the firearm that perched on the wall. I was dismayed to even consider this being a threat to whatever was out there, but I had no choice. Bags, bottles, and bullets were chucked together and tossed onto the bed to compile. It was only when I fumbled for my keys that my darting eyes were halted by the white flicker of a machine across the room from me. I stood there for an awfully long time.

No, I tried to reason with myself. *That's not... that's not right.* I pushed myself to my window to check for a car that might have pulled in. Nothing. I almost had to wrest my head just to bear looking back to my computer. Each step I made towards the machine was slow and weighty, as if both my legs were bound to ball-and-chains. It took over a minute for me to practically fall into the chair at my desk, and fully read the message displayed on the screen.

One notification, from a friend: 'I have come to meet you. Do not be afraid.'

Halloween Night

MARCELLA MARIA DE A. L. ROCHA

*M*y name is Maya Grey, and I am a shifter. It was Halloween night, the only night of the year when I could show my true self, the animal inside of me. Tonight was no different. It had been 20 years of my life since the night I first transformed. I went into my backyard, as usual, breathing in the cold air. My tiger was feeling restless, but tonight it was worse than usual. It was like she was pushing me out of my skin. I tied my hair in a high bun; it could become difficult during the shift. My hair, like my mother's, was long, curly and black like the feathers of a raven. The coincidence of that is that my mother was a raven shifter, and my father was a tiger shifter. Unfortunately, I took after him. My tiger is powerful, fierce and a little moody on a good day, but she is a constant reminder of my anger towards him for leaving my mother and I to die alone without the protection of the pack.

My mother is my heroine; I grew up mirroring her actions. After my father left us, we became loners, and my mother fought very hard to protect us. But I was the one who found us a new home, a new pack, a sanctuary where she could relax rest and spend the rest of her days in peace. I remembered moving into our new home like it was yesterday.

Mum's eyes were red from crying, as always. But after five years of living in the street, I finally found something for us. She might regret putting me in this position, but she was weakened because of the breaking of the bond between her and my sperm donor. I had to fight dirty, but I got enough money and connections over the years to be able to buy the house. As mum walked inside her new two-storey house, which she had always dreamed of having, with a big white fence, and rustic bricks. I moved to only two streets away so we could always see each other.

I became a weapon any pack would kill to have; everyone fought over me and made high proposals to get me into their pack. I chose the one that I knew no one would go after, especially not my father's old pack. There are many packs. Some are strictly one kind of shifter, and others are open to anyone with power no matter the shifter kind.

However, now was not the time to think of what I had done to arrive where I am or even think about my loser of a father. I could feel the pain of the transition; my nails were sharpening. I undressed and left my clothes folded on the small table that I had put on the edge of the forest that connected to my house. I examined my surroundings, the trees and bushes around my property gave me some privacy for my change from my neighbours as I changed. My skin shivered as the cold wind passed through me, and I let my inner animal free.

She was happy to run free for in the night, jumping from tree to tree, and marking her territory. As my tiger went to jump on the last branch, her nostrils expanded and she smelled *him*, another like her. But he was hiding from her, as it was waited for a moment to attack and submit her. She would not let that happen. She was no submissive little kitten; she was an alpha. My mother and I got kicked out of our old pack because my sperm donor left us there alone, and the other males wanted to control my mother. But she was a raven and she was not going to be put in a cage. She trusted in my strength and leadership, so we travelled the world together until it was time to settle.

My tiger shakes her head as she tries to clear the anger forming from the memories clouding her mind. As she prepared to jump, her companion attacked her. It was a white tiger no less, but she was prepared. She went to the left as he clashed with the trunk of a tree. While he tried to recover, she pounced for his back, but he anticipated the attack, and they clashed paws and fangs drawing blood. Her animal was determined to win, as she pierced her claws through his chest. As he tried to take a step back, he mis-stepped and fell to the ground.

My tiger went after him and started to circle him as her prey. The white tiger transformed into a man, naked as the day he was born. As he stood up and fixed his golden eyes on her. After a moment, his lips curved into a strange smile as he spoke.

'It is polite to shift back to human when your opponent does.'

My tiger huffed at him for his audacity and continued circling him, waiting for him to make a mistake so she could attack. As she locked eyes with him once again, her tiger froze. A peculiar scent wafted into her nostrils causing a strange race of emotions to run through me. *Mate. My mate.* The yin to my yang was there standing right in front of me. And he attacked me! He tried to make me submit! As I looked at his face, I realised that he was not surprised or showing any kind of emotion of that always shows when mates find each other. I got control of my tiger, and we moved behind one of the trees where I had hidden a stash of clothes. I shifted back and began getting dressed as *my mate* spoke again.

'My name is Aron if you are wondering,' he purred. 'What is your name?'

'Are you not going to tell me your name?' Aron called after me. My mind was still getting together about the whole 'mate' thing that I almost missed him speaking again.

'You have a cute tiger,' he began, 'but she is not very friendly. My tiger only wanted to say hi.'

Walls of Fire: Infernal Bonds

Emily Home

S taring up at the elegant woman in his family portrait overlooking the entry hall, he was reminded of the last time he'd seen her. A faint glow emitted from the intricately designed patterns and carefully sculpted runes of the arcane sigil that had been carved into the ceiling. Bathing the room in a gentle magenta, it acted merely to break the darkness. Comforting it may have been, it did little to lull him into slumber. What had started as a gentle shower had suddenly churned into a vicious storm that thrashed his window and chilled him deep with shrieking, eerie howls. He sat up, unable to shake a creeping sense of dread.

This is stupid, he wrapped his blanket tightly around his shoulders, *only babies are scared of storms.*

A tiny spark from the looming darkness caught his eye. Squinting, he tried to make out any discernible shapes through the waterfall streaming down the window panes. Sure enough, there it was again; a pinprick glow flickered vainly against the raging storm.

What madman is outside in this weather?

He pressed his hand against the cold glass, shoved it open against the gale, and focused his vision. A figure, clinging desperately to an oversized shroud with one hand and a whipping lantern in the other, shambled towards the towering forest beyond the property border. Slicking his soaked hair out of his eyes, he contemplated calling out to his father. He never took kindly to trespassers. He froze however, as a violent gust ripped the shroud from the figure's hands and revealed a tall, slender woman with hair tangling wildly in the wind.

'Mum?' he muttered. Resigning to losing her protective shroud, the woman clutched herself tightly and continued forward.

'Mum!' the wind drowned his call. Yet the figure hesitated for a brief moment, before dashing the final yards to the forest edge.

'Mum! Mum!' his screams broke through his throat as hot tears stung his sodden cheeks.

He remembered that night with an intense disgust that twisted his stomach into a running knot. At five years old he had been the centrepiece of the painting, presented proudly by his father–a tall daemon man with deep crimson skin and ornately decorated horns–on his right, and his mother–a slender, beautiful elven woman with long, black windswept hair–on his left. The next night his dear mother slunk away into a blustering storm, never to be seen again.

'Take me with you,' he whispered to the canvas, placing a gentle hand over his mother's.

'Elzare!' He jumped at the booming voice, quickly retracting his hand. The towering figure of his father sauntered towards him. 'How many times must I tell you, child,' his deep mellow voice made Elzare's stomach churn, 'the oil from your hands will fade the paint.'

'I'm sorry, sir,' he avoided his father's gaze. He reached out and gently grasped his son's horn, stroking the tip with his thumb. Elzare's jaw tightened in a grimace.

'Not to worry,' he chuckled, removing his hand, 'you ought to be getting ready for your ceremony.' An anxious twang tugged at Elzare's chest. It was his tenth birthday, which made him of indoctrination age; he'd hoped his father had forgotten. He'd forgotten every birthday for five years, yet an excited spark flickered in his father's golden eyes at the mention of this ceremony.

He would never forget, Elzare determined.

'We wouldn't want to keep the Great One waiting, would we?'

'No sir.' His father's gaze bore into his back as he ushered himself back to his room. The ceremonial garb he was meant to wear loomed over the cramped space from its spot on his closet door. It had been taunting him since the day his father brought it home, reminding him of his impending destiny.

Later in the evening, there came a gentle rapping at his door. Before he could utter a word, it flung open to reveal a finely dressed human man, the manor's trusted butler. 'Lord Dharris has sent for you, Master Elzare,' he slicked back his salt and pepper hair, his tired face drenched in sweat. 'Are you prepared?' Elzare glanced at his reflection. He wore a fine, red silken robe edged with thick, golden strips that glittered under the chandelier's warm light. He nodded silently. The butler sighed and knelt in front of him. 'Your chains are twisted.' Gently, he unlatched the fragile, gold chains holding the robes closed.

'I don't care, Thaddeus,' he tried to pull away.

'Nonsense,' Thaddeus ran his nails along the chains before relatching them. 'This is a big day for you.' Elzare stared into the butler's weary eyes. Anxiety gripped his stomach; something about his eyes that night unsettled him. They were as gentle as always, yet laced with an emotion Elzare hadn't seen in him before. Something was troubling him. Had it been sadness? Guilt? Regret? He never asked. 'Come,' Thaddeus said, standing tall, 'Lord Dharris awaits your presence.' He outstretched his faintly creased palm and Elzare—with brief hesitation—lightly grasped his index finger.

The journey into the basement took an eternity under the overbearing weight of silence. Thaddeus heaved full iron shelves away from the back wall whilst Elzare held a small, flickering candle. In amongst the miscellaneous clutter, Elzare recognised the old, dusty form of the synthetic Winter Star tree tossed carelessly in the far corner. The last time he had seen it was the winter before his mother left. The same decorations still clung to its scratchy branches. 'There,' Thaddeus grunted, pulling the last shelf away. 'Are you ready?' he asked again. Elzare started up at a large, rusted iron door that was padlocked shut with a thick steel chain. It contrasted enormously against the smooth ash brick walls of the basement; he was shocked he'd never noticed it before. Thaddeus raised an eyebrow, waiting for an answer.

Elzare took a deep breath. 'Okay.'

The Chronicles of Sun Gazer: Return of Death Bringer

HAYLEY CHERRY

*S*he quickly darted through the burning corridor, checking each room for the helpless hostages of the fire. The calling out became less frequent, as their hope of survival faded, as did the oxygen in their lungs. Sun Gazer quickly ascended through the fire escape. As she cleared the first floor, the voices got closer. She made it to the next floor, knowing this was the final one. As the voices grew weak, Sun Gazer lost her tracks and struggled to pinpoint exactly where they were.

'Keep calling out to me!' Sun Gazer yelled, 'I will make my way to you!'

Weak, coughing voices cried, hopeful that they were getting out alive. However, this sparked a deep rage in the fire. The intensity of the flames increased, as the furniture once standing peacefully now crumbled into a pile of charcoal. Being exposed to the heat for so long, Sun Gazer began to feel the heat seep through her super-suit and onto her skin. Though it didn't cause her pain, it did give her a feeling of unusual discomfort.

She shielded her eyes from the glare of the fire around her, its attempts at holding her back, failing. As Sun Gazer trenched through the burning building, the trembling cries of the trapped family got closer and clearer. She reached what seemed to be a dead end, however, discovered a pile of burnt rubble in front of a door. The dying pleas of the family were coming from the other side. She began shovelling the rubble away from the door. Each touch burned a layer of her protective gloves. She could feel the sweat drip down from her face, her skin melting from the excessive heat of the fire. She realised her suit may not be so fire-proof, as the heat began to prickle her skin. It caused her to lightly wince at the feeling. Sun Gazer ignored what was happening to her body and continued to clear the rubble until she could finally see the door handle.

'Step away from the door!' she yelled, 'I'm going to kick it open!'

Once she received an all-clear, she got into position and rammed her body into the door.

It didn't budge. Sun Gazer winced as the side of her body prickled from the heat of the impact. She went again, the door still not budging.

Sun Gazer could feel the heat get to her, overwhelming her mind. It tried to make her fall victim to its fiery rage, as it did with its hostages. However, she ignored its persistence and rammed her body into the door again. This time, the door fell through and crumbled into jagged wooden pieces.

A glint of hope sparkled in the family's eyes as they looked at her in awe. In a flash, Sun Gazer hurried to where the father sat, embracing his two young children protectively. They sat helpless. However, the father stood his ground—fighting every bone in his body to run and hide—to protect his children. Sun Gazer took the unconscious little girl from her father's grasp and cupped her in her arms. She noticed the child's face was red and dirtied, the heat and smoke painted over her like dust.

'Follow me closely,' Sun Gazer commanded. The father nodded in agreement.

They both ran out of the burning room and into the heated hallway. The fire was raging its blistering blaze. This time it was much angrier and did its best to reach the family with its smouldering fingertips. Yet, they all slipped past its attempts to burn them and made it to the window. Sun Gazer looked down outside the window and noticed people scattered everywhere around the street, watching and recording. The firefighters had a giant, inflated platform hoisted and ready beneath the window. She turned around and reached for the other young girl still in her father's hands.

'I will take these two down safely and come back for you … I promise,' she said.

The father hesitated for a moment; his eyes glinted with fear. However, he swiftly handed his second child over to Sun Gazer, who accepted her, along with her sister. She coddled both tightly and leapt out of the window. She caught a gust of wind with her feet and gently glided onto the ground. Paramedics quickly rushed towards her and grabbed the children from her grasp. They brought them to their stretchers and pushed them into the ambulance vehicles where they began their medical processes. She sighed in relief and examined the blotches of burnt skin all over her arms.

She watched as the panicked man from before quickly rushed to his children's sides and held them tightly. He shed tears of relief. The police began to usher people away from the road as fire trucks finally arrived. Sun Gazer turned around and saw the father standing in the building, 12 floors from the ground, desperately clinging to the edge. She quickly jumped up into the air and made her way to him. Just as she reached him, she heard an instant *swoosh* and a *crack*.

The father's expression widened with shock for a moment and then softened as he went limp and suddenly fell out of the window. Sun Gazer swept up and caught him and gently guided his unconscious body to the ground. She heard screaming and commotion in the background, however, it all went into a blur. She saw the father dead, the one she couldn't save. She smelt the iron from the fresh blood that spilled from his chest, as the liquid ooze dripped down onto her hands. She saw the familiar arrow planted clean through his back, pin-pointed perfectly through his heart.

Sun Gazer thought of all the possibilities of this happening. This one caught her off-guard. Her heart sank and her limbs trembled. Sitting in a growing pool of blood, she reached down to the small, pink note that stuck snugly at the tip of the arrow.

Archmage

CERYS BARNES

'*L*in, what are you doing?'

I poked my head out from under the table. My father, who I'd only met a few days ago, stood there with a small smile playing about his face.

'I wish I had a good answer, but in reality I'm not entirely sure what I'm doing either,' I responded.

My father snorted in amusement. I could only imagine what he was seeing: his nearly sixteen-year-old son, a mirror image of himself, sitting under the table with assorted weapons, tools, and magic tomes all over the floor surrounding him.

Of course, he'd only found out my very existence a few days ago. Suddenly having a son would be a major adjustment.

'Your father and I are not divorced, Lin-Lin,' my mother always said, growing up. 'Nor did he abandon us. We were merely separated.'

'Separated?' I'd always ask.

'Yes. Separated.' She'd always go into story mode, even though it was the truth. 'There we were, on the frontlines, fighting off a horde of giant, evil monsters. We won, but us, alongside many others, were greatly injured. Your father and I had been stationed at opposite ends of the battlefield, and—'

'But why didn't he come find us?' I asked.

She'd huff a laugh. I always interrupted her at that same spot. 'Believe me, I know he tried. He's a very stubborn man. He wouldn't have given up looking for us. But… he might be surprised when he does find us.'

'Why?'

'Because he'd find out about you, pumpkin. I didn't know I was pregnant with you

until I was recovering from my injuries,' she'd say, ruffling my white hair.

She'd waited for my father, all those years. Her family were not exactly supportive of her being a single mother. Children before marriage was frowned upon by them. However, my mother never paid their opinions any mind. There was only one opinion of theirs she'd cared about— the secret she'd hidden from them her entire life.

I remember as a child, reading about it. Across cover to cover of history books, it was always said that humanity was divided into two groups. United, yet separate. These two groups consisted of Ciphers—non-magic users, and Espers—magic users. It didn't matter if you were born into a family of magic or not; sometimes that seed grew regardless.

Amongst Ciphers, there were those who were strongly anti-magic, and believed sorcerers should be restricted and monitored, as their only purpose was to drive back the demons and monsters threatening the world.

My mother and myself were both Espers. As was my father.

Unfortunately, there are some Espers that have their magic change part of their body. This usually occurs in the eyes, resulting in an unnatural colour.

When I awoke my magic at four, I developed the bodily change I couldn't hide. The only solution to hide it from my family was saying I had an eye condition and was extremely sensitive to light. The *doctor* had prescribed me sunglasses, which I was to also wear indoors.

Because my family hates sorcerers so much, my mother couldn't get me any tutors to help me learn magic. She herself taught me what magic she knew, alongside purchasing me magic textbooks. I'd always pounce on the book as soon as she gave it to me, hungrily devouring the words.

The problem was the more I used magic, the more my eyes changed colour … and the more difficult it became to hide what I was at core. Originally my eyes were a deep brown, but over the years, they began changing to a vivid orange.

After sixteen years, my mother and father had reunited in a chance encounter. He'd found us, just as she said he would, even if it was by accident. My father's name is Ren Noctis. He worked as an Imperial Weaponsmith—one of the Espers in charge of making all the magical and enchanted weapons for the Imperial Army. These such weapons were then used to fight the monsters and demons that plagued this world.

But despite his position, he'd dropped everything that he was doing once he'd learned of my existence. I now lived with him and was adjusting to my new life. My mother remained back in my hometown but would eventually join us here.

'—Lin? Earth to Lin,' My father waved his hand in front of my face, 'Are you in there?'

I jolted back to reality.

'Sorry,' I said sheepishly. 'Did you say something?'

He grinned, then ruffled my hair. I shied away, but that made him do it more. Our laughter echoed throughout the room, eventually dying down.

'Well, since neither of us know what you're doing,' my father said, 'Would you like to come with me to a meeting with some certain nosy bastards who think I've finally lost all my marbles and am imagining you?'

'...I don't see anything wrong with losing your marbles.'

'Neither do I, but if you start imagining your own child, then there's definitely a problem,' he mused. 'I want to prove to them I have at least some sanity left.'

I hid my smile. 'Is that all?'

'All of what?' he asked innocently.

'Is that the only reason why you want me to come with you?'

He raised an eyebrow. 'If this is you trying to get me to admit that I want to show my son off, then yes, this is me attempting to do so.'

'Do you want to come or not?' he asked with a smile.

'Of course.' I finally scrambled out from underneath the table, neatly stacking the tomes about magic to the side.

Despite managing to not knock my head painfully against the table, I tripped over the weapons I'd had under the table, and somehow managed to knock my sunglasses off. I watched as they clattered to the floor, bouncing not once, not twice, but three times before coming to rest at my father's feet. He bent down to pick them up.

'Careful now. Don't want to break these.' He straightened to his full height and examined them. 'Good! Not a scratch. Here you go.' It was only when my father extended his arm to hand them back to me that he caught sight of my eyes.

He instantly tucked the glasses into his pocket and stepped forward. He cupped my face with both hands, examining my face.

'Lin. What colour were your eyes when you came back with me?'

I blinked. '… Bright orange?'

'That's what I thought.' The look on his face was dead serious. 'You mentioned that you still wore your sunglasses by habit. No wonder you haven't noticed it yet.'

'Noticed what?'

My father conjured up a piece of silver metal in an instant. He held it up for me. I peered at my reflection. My eyes were now a bright, metallic gold.

'Golden eyes…' he murmured. 'The signature colour of the sorcerer capable of overthrowing, destroying, or shaping the world as they pleased.' His voice was quiet.

Destroyer of demons. Descendant of dragons.

A savior of humanity.

Archmage.

Kill Your God

RHYS MOORE

*W*hen I was young, I set out to kill my god.

I wore the white cloth garb befitting my holy adventure. My mother and sister had freshly bleached it with the white petals of the Hartseer flower, and so it glowed in the sun. As I walked, it emitted the scent of plump, ripe stone fruit. My broad sword hung in a fur sheath slung over my shoulder. My father had belted the sword into being over an ancient flame that no longer burned.

I wore no shoes, needed no crown, beheld no other opinion.

I was steadfast as I turned my back on the plentiful fields and ashen mountain of my homeland and set out for the far-off forest.

The trek was simple; a trail forged deep and wide by those who had dared to tread before me. All those simple men, unknowing and unwavering. The trail died as I reached the wall of wild trees. They grew through the sky and sat as broad as ten men. I stood as a speck before them. The scent of orange and tarberry flowed out in an alluring breeze. I swigged a mouthful of water from my pilgrim bottle, my fingers delighting in the soft, short fur that covered the cured leather.

I wrenched through the forest. The trees' lecherous arms stretched out above me, creating a canopy that allowed only the occasional belt of light amongst obsidian. I tripped and tumbled over roots and weeds—brandishing my sword to clear a path but finding little success. At night, I perched on ripples of stone and scrub, unable to see my hands before my eyes. The berry breeze grew constant, and its bouquet blew stronger each day I burrowed further into the forest. Wild whispers wove through that sweet, soft wind, but I steeled myself against the scents and sounds.

Late one day, I came across a cliff face that stretched above the trees. The canopy thinned in response to the rock, allowing a faint orange light to caress its strangely supple surface. It gently oscillated under my tentative hand as I checked for footing. The light was beginning to pass.

Eager to evade the dark void and whispers of previous nights, I took my broad sword and heaved it into the stone. It gave easily, like peeling through ripe fruit, before jarring harshly a third of the way up. I hung off my sword to check its support. Confident it would hold, I pulled my feet up to just below the blade and then jumped as I pulled the sword out and stuck it in at the zenith of my leap. I kept my head neutral to stay my balance and focus. I continued upward and with each leap my sword delved deeper. Light drenched my shoulders and blinded me as the canopy gave way.

I do not know how long I climbed. My neck felt as though it had been soldered to my skull, my shoulders spat at my name and my legs begged for death. A soft breeze blew the same sweet scent from below the canopy and on it rode an unintelligible whisper.

Then I fell.

My final strike had hit air, but my blade served me one more time—catching into the strange rock as I dropped. The precipice lay a fathom above me. My hands burned. The breeze returned.

'Relent,' it whispered across my neck.

No.

I pulled my feet upward one more time. My knees made small popping sounds, and my hips creaked open.

I leapt with only one thought, one goal, one chance.

Do not die.

I woke with hot air flying through my throat. I flung up and coughed out sand, but no spittle would form to dislodge the grit from my palette. I searched for my bottle but found nothing.

My sword! I began to rise slowly, but my vision churned, and I fell to my knees.

Crawl.

The sun scorched overhead as the sand seared my skin. I reached the edge of the cliff and peered over. My sword was still there, lodged in the rock up to the hilt. I balanced my chest and arms over the edge, nearly tipping over twice. At last, I grasped the handle of my sword and pulled. Only a short stump of blade remained. I had thought it biting deeper when in fact it had been breaking. I dropped it in disgust, and it sunk quickly into the abyss below. Tears tore at my eyes.

I crawled away from the edge. For hours I scraped through the sand with an acrid mouth and on the verge of hallucination. The lapping of water caught my ears and sprung my limbs along. I came to a small dune, and with my lips burning, body screaming, and soul-shaking, I crested it. The cool, solid sand was a relief, and I let my body roll down the dune's natural curve until I fell into the water. It was cold and fresh and invigorating. The relief made me laugh and cry.

I lost all sense of being.

I lay naked on the shore, meditating to the lapping of water, the clean, dry scent of sand, and the cleansing rays of the sun. Then, a familiar fruity breeze stirred my senses and set goosebumps upon my flesh. The whisper was now a deep, feminine voice.

'Relent,' the voice said. 'Look into the water.'

I obeyed.

I met the water. In it, I saw my father.

'Take me back,' I pleaded.

'Even a god cannot turn back time,' the voice replied. 'I am sorry.'

'Women seek retribution. Men seek forgiveness.'

'Where have I heard that?'

'From those you left behind.'

'The ones I loved.'

'Men show love through violence.'

The sun started to set. In the distance, I could hear someone swinging wildly in the dark. I closed my eyes. I exhaled.

I relented.

The Graveyard Shift

LOUANA SUTCLIFFE

*E*very night, mist crept up from the river and smothered the adjacent highway in its damp breath. Its fingers reached through the paperbark and eucalypt scrub and inched up the offramp from the highway to the Lonely Dingo, until the servo was an eerie island in a sea of pale gloom.

Chris acknowledged the mist like you do a neighbour you've known for years. Not one you much like, but one you know well. It signified his 9 to 5 at the Dingo starting in earnest, always making its appearance not long after the kids at the Hungry Jacks next door closed up. Sometimes they'd bring in leftover fries or the dregs of the soft-serve machine and wish him a quiet, uneventful night.

Then he'd be alone.

Just a book and whoever was taking the graveyard shift on Triple J for company. And the mist.

Tonight was fries and soft serve. Chris shifted on the stool behind the counter and dunked a limp fry in the melted ice-cream pooled in the bottom of the tub. He opened the book at the dog-eared page. It was the latest he'd swiped from Mandy's bookshelf, one of the less spooky

197

Stephen King novels she owned. Less supernatural bullshit, more detective work. Mandy had bounced off this one a bit. Didn't like the realism. Wasn't as scary, she said.

Chris flipped the page. He found monsters in a crime novel to be scarier than vampires. One exists. The other doesn't. Besides, he liked solving the mystery alongside the literary detective. Or before. He'd have made a good detective, Chris reckoned. In another life. If he hadn't dropped out of school at Year 10 to pursue that apprenticeship and realised bricklaying was a prick of a job. *Should've listened to the old man.* Not like working night shift at a servo was much better, but at least it was easy work. Only had to deal with the odd psycho from across the bridge out west, or the occasional truckies mind-fried on the unholy trinity of caffeine, coke and no fuckin' sleep.

A low rumble groaned through the Triple J host's monologue. Chris raised his eyes, over the shelves of snacks and magazines glimmering under cold bright lights and out the condensation-blurred window.

Twin cones cut through the mist sea and angled up the ramp. The remainder of the cab's lights flashed like a riot scene in an action movie as the semi-trailer skirted around the illuminated fuel pumps and angled toward the far end of the carpark.

Chris nudged the dial on the radio up and went back to his book. Not unusual, truckies parking in the dark. The Dingo was known to be a quiet place for a few hours of shut eye. The Triple J host's monologue had been replaced with a song Chris struggled to place. It was older, with a man's deep voice and piano that prickled his skin with every unnerving note. He turned the page and tried to focus. The detective was attending another murder scene—

A door slammed and Chris jolted. The book toppled to the counter. The truckdriver avoided the fuel pump lights and stalked toward the servo shop, a darker stain on the moonless night. The piano serenaded his footsteps, closer to the sliding glass door that Chris opened with the button push below the counter. Damp air sighed through the door, cold as the man's stare. He clocked the security camera behind the counter and raised his chin to Chris.

'Evening, mate,' Chris said. He fought the urge to reach for the cricket bat that lived under the counter. *Get a grip, dude.* Too many murder mysteries.

The man strode around the shelves, a feral dog circling a street cat. His boot heels cut over the music like gunshots in the dark. An alarm bell jangled in Chris' brain.

At the shelf by the drinks fridge the man stopped. 'Quiet night?'

'Always.'

The man smirked and continued his lap of the shop. His eyes flicked toward the camera again. On the radio, the piano swelled with intensity.

The man brought his goods to the counter. Chris stiffened. *You've gotta be fuckin' with me …* Duct tape. Nylon rope. A Stanley knife in one of those packets that requires a damn Stanley knife to open. And a 1.25L Pepsi.

'That all?' The nylon rope was slippery in Chris' palms. He thrust it in front of the scanner, then froze, eyes on the man's right hand. There, on the webbing between thumb and forefinger, a red, indented semi-circle and the smear of something pink. *Lipstick.* The man's hand disappeared below the counter and the lines between his cold eyes deepened. The rope scanned again.

'Shit, sorry.' Chris fumbled with the register screen. Sweat dampened the collar of his polo.

'Good?'

He flinched and glanced up. 'What?'

The man gestured to the book on the counter with a crinkled 50 dollar note.

Chris gaped at the lurid cover. 'Yeah, it's good,' he croaked.

'Do they catch the killer?' The words dripped mockery. The register drawer clanged. On the radio, the piano surged to a jarring climax.

Chris pushed the man's items and change across the counter and met the cold, glittering eyes. His pulse thrummed against the rope and roll of duct tape. 'Yeah,' he said. 'Yeah, they do.'

The man smirked again, grabbed his items and swaggered through the door. He took the dark path back to the cab of the truck and disappeared around the far side. The truck door slammed again, then the engine roared through the night and the huge vehicle lurched toward the servo's exit.

And left, across the bridge to the west.

The mist swallowed the truck and the Dingo fell silent—just the radio, and Chris' blood pounding in his ears. He glanced at the book, then reached for the phone.

Eyes in the Hallways

BIANCA CAVANAGH

I'm watching you. I sway my head from side to side. *Surely, this is a joke.* Reaching up, I swipe at the piece of paper taped to my front door with the mysterious message scrawled on it. When I flip the page over, nothing is on the other side. I glance around; every door in this apartment complex looks the same, but mine is the only one with a note. I stash it away in my pocket and retrieve my key. *Wait … what if someone is inside?* I spend a few seconds glaring at the doorknob. Taking a deep breath, I slide the key into the lock. As I turn it, the door creaks back; I pad through and close it behind me. I ball my hands into fists, realising I have nothing to protect myself. Like a soldier preparing for battle, I brace myself for what might come.

One, two, three. In my haste to catch an intruder, I storm into the bedroom and then the bathroom. I return to the entryway near the living room and kitchen. *No one is here.* A laugh escapes my lips. Haha! *How stupid of me to think someone had broken in.* I slip the briefcase off my shoulder and set it on the kitchen bench. Reaching into my pocket, I remove the note and toss it in the bin.

Buzz. Buzz. Like popcorn kernels in the microwave, I jump. *There better not be a text to go with that letter.* I draw my phone out of my briefcase slower than a convoy of snails travelling through peanut butter. It's a text from Tate: *Hey Jack, working late tonight, see you when I get home.* I rest one hand on my heart and type back: *I'll wait up. Drive safe.*

'Hey there, gorgeous,' I say as Tate drags her feet inside, coffee in hand. Her hair is a fierce lion's mane, sticking out in wild directions.

'Hello,' she replies in a weary monotone. I feel the famous butterflies as she strolls over to the couch to kiss me. Her kiss is like a gentle explosion, setting off underground minefields beneath my skin's surface. A smile sneaks out of the corner of her mouth, and her cheeks turn pink.

'How was your day?' I ask as Tate wanders over to the bin. *Uh Oh.*

Long,' she replies before spotting the note, preparing to dump her cup. 'What is this?' she asks, picking it out. *I should have taken the rubbish out.* 'I'm watching you,' she reads, her brows furrowed as she turns to face me. I bob my shoulders, hiding the panic inside me. 'Well?' she presses. I rise from my spot on the couch and pace over to her, running my hands through my hair to seem relaxed.

'It was taped to the front door when I got home,' I reply. There was silence for a second or two, the gap between lightning and thunder. 'It's probably just a prank; nothing to worry about.' She gawks at me like I have just declared myself a flying cow. 'I checked the house to be safe,' I add, hoping to comfort her. After dropping the note on the bench, Tate tosses her cup into the bin.

'You checked the house expecting to find someone here? What would you do, fling files from your faux leather bag at their face?'

'No, I …' I don't finish my sentence because I have never physically fought anyone; I was fooling myself into believing I could compete against someone else. Tate doesn't expect an answer; instead, she places her thumb loosely between her top and bottom teeth.

A few seconds pass, and she starts pacing, 'Okay, hear me out.'

I roll my eyes, knowing she will go off on a tangent. *She always thinks outside the box and vents her thoughts to me daily, even if they seem crazy. I love her for that.*

'Someone could be taking note of our clothes, mimicking our movements to try and frame us for a robbery … Or the government is doing experiments on the public and has chosen us as their next targets …'

'Tate,' I announce, trying to get her attention.

'Or someone is obsessed with one or both of us if they are into that kind of thing; perhaps they broke in and installed hidden cameras.' I felt a chill radiate down my spine just thinking about it. 'Or …'

'Tate, sweetie, stop,' I say, jolting her back to reality with a slight shake, 'let's not jump to conclusions.'

Erupting with fury, she stomps towards the door. 'We cannot stay here, Jack.'

'Where are we going to go?' Tate faces me and lifts her hands in the air before lowering them to her sides.

'A friend's, a hotel, anywhere but here.' Snapping eye contact, Tate forces the front door open and stands transfixed, peering at the other side of it. I move towards her, like metal to a magnet—*another note*. A wave of nausea washes over me and sweat springs out in beads on my brows. I shift my gaze to Tate, who stares back at me with owl-like eyes. Pulling myself together, I take a long breath and remove the piece of paper again taped to the door. Tate grasps the opposite side, allowing us to read it together; her hands shake in a trembling rhythm. Three words are scribbled on it: *Sorry, wrong apartment.* Tate and I flick our heads to inspect the apartment across from ours. Their note is identical to our first one: *I'm watching you.*

'Wait…' Tate releases the paper and holds up a finger, locking eyes with me.

As if reading her thoughts, I say, 'Someone is stalking our building.' Tate's arms grow with goosebumps. I fling my arms around her, embracing her tight, my head buried in her golden curls. *We're moving.*

Everyday Heroes

ETHAN RACH

*T*ears swelled in my eyes as I began to speak. *Come on, mate, get on with it. Do it for Eric.*

'Good morning, everyone. Thank you for coming in today. My name is David Greene and I was asked on behalf of the Winters family to contribute my own thoughts on Eric and what he was truly like.' *Deep breaths, mate.*

'Eric Winters, the teacher, the role model, the hero. Routine had become his drive, something that he longed for all his life and finally achieved—a modicum of normality, a sense of belonging. From his morning swim on the beaches of Caloundra to his after-school rush with cars bumper to bumper along the highway. Eric wouldn't have changed it for a soul—he lived for it, and when times such as these were so set on change, would it be so bad to try to keep it altogether?

'At a quarter of a century, many things had already changed not just for Eric and his life but for all our lives. Here, radicalisation was the theme of the decade, and it was evident wherever you looked. From the increased police presence in schools to the regular heavily armed foot patrols up and down the esplanade. Australia was going through change. It wasn't an overnight sensation, either; this fundamental change in society served as a slow, painful burn that seeped itself into the everyday doings of man, woman and child. Going back as early as the September 11 attacks, to as late as the Wieambilla shootings, change was imminent. Perpetrators such as these wished for a re-do, to be done with the old and in with the new. But not for Eric, for he loved his life and the people in it. Standing at over six-foot three, with his long, wavy dark hair, emboldened by an athletic build, one might think Eric wanted to be outstanding, but this was never the case. Eric was the sort of man who embraced the systematic function of society, to do his part, to help whoever and whenever he can. A man of the people—a brother to us all.

'I think of that day often, when my life changed forever. A Friday like many others, sun shining, waves crashing, sand burning. Another day in paradise. It was as if it was too perfect.

'I remember saying to Eric, as the kids rushed from the bus, "Day for it, don't you think, Mr Winters?"

'"Yeah, Dave, it's a beauty, love to see it." Although being the youngest of the group, Eric had already situated himself as a leader among his teaching team. However, as a teacher one should always expect the unexpected—especially working with children.

'As the kids blitzed out, everyone had seemed to be having a blast. Cricket was being played, footies were being kicked, staff were complaining about admin. That's when we heard it. Faint at the start, like a buzzing of a bee but then it grew louder and nearer, up until it could've only been one thing. Gunfire.

'Chaos. Then destruction ensued, as the once peaceful surroundings suddenly descended into unrecognisable madness. Dozens of everyday people rushed away from the oncoming wave of carnage as I stood there frozen. Four gunmen adorned in dark camo clothing, packing an arsenal of weaponry between them. They were death incarnate, like a dark fog washing over the beach, bringing nothing but dread and despair. No warning, no indicator, just death. The once bustling esplanade of our home descended into an uncontrolled catastrophe. Where were the kids? Where was Eric? I tried to move, but fear had struck me down— fear and cowardice. I knew I had to get the kids back on the bus, but it was as if my feet had gone limp and I couldn't help but watch as the men drew nearer. They're going to kill the kids.

'That's when I saw Eric. Our Eric. Our everyday hero. As I stood there cowering, Eric was out there leading. Bringing child after child back to the bus in droves. At times carrying three or four at once. It was something to behold, as if he had no care for his own life, but only for the children. By the time I was out of the trance I remember Ms Blake standing next to me, saying, "Get up, Dave, the kids need us." As I was thrust into danger I looked to Eric as my role model—to act not think. Time seemed to move even slower as I reached for the kids around me. They began flocking to the bus en masse. But where was Eric?

'As the police arrived ready to send death back into hell, that's when I spotted him—under a tree, hand on his stomach, blood all over him. I remember screaming, "Fucking hell! Eric! Eric mate, hold on. I'll go get someone!"

'That's when he spoke, "The kids, Dave … are the kids safe … are they alright?"

"'Yeah mate, you saved them. All of them. You're a hero."

"Just doing … what I thought was right … Look after them, Dave, for the both of us." As the glow of his eyes faded I will never forget the last words Eric ever spoke to me, as if they were branded into my heart.

'As Eric died his words have never left me. He died thinking he was just like every other man. This couldn't have been further from the truth—he was the hero in all our lives.

'Now, two weeks have passed since his death, and the evidence of his time here on this earth is clear for everyone. Over 1000 people have attended his service today and I thank every one of you. From parents of the children he saved, officers who witnessed his heroism, to Ms Blake and I. 1000 people who recognised Eric as not just an everyday person, but an everyday hero. We love you, Eric.'

The Lake

LINNEA FRENCH

*A*s a child, my world was steeped in magic, where the vibrant green grass of summer would transform into a frozen winter wonderland for three months each year. I would watch as the lake I grew up beside would gradually solidify, its surface morphing from a gentle ripple into an icy expanse, beckoning and treacherous all at once.

When I was younger, a girl from my class vanished one day without a trace. Later, I found out she had gone to the lake to play. It was late February, that time when the sun started to weaken winter's hold, causing the ice to thin and the ground to soften. She had fallen through when the ice could no longer bear her growing weight. She froze to death in the icy water. My parents told me it was a peaceful end, that she felt no pain. At the time I believed them, now I can't help but wonder if that was really true.

Those memories clung to me as I grew older. The tales my parents spun about the ice were etched into my being, impossible to forget. My brother, five years older, always made sure to follow me whenever I ventured onto the frozen lake. He was my guardian, keeping me safe from the lurking dangers our parents warned us about. When the sun dipped low on the horizon, he'd ruffle my hair, our breath misting in the cold air as we made our way back to the warmth and safety of home.

When the phone call came, I listened in silence, my breath steady as my parents told the story. When the line went dead, I sat there, waiting for the wave of emotions to hit. But how could they when my parents were wrong? It wasn't even the new year yet. Of all people, he would have been careful. He knew the rules, the warnings. No, they had to be wrong, there was no other explanation I could comprehend.

My brother, just out of college, looked so peaceful, almost as if he were sleeping, when I said my final goodbye. The service was filled with people who loved him, painting his life as though it were a fairytale. A wonderful person, student, son and brother, taken from us far too soon. Everyone around me was sombre, crying and praying, but I couldn't shed a tear. I was too angry, too lost in my own turmoil to even begin to express my grief.

I sat in those church pews thinking about all the times Mum and Dad had sat us down and told us the rules. Never go to the lake without each other, never after January, always check the thickness of the ice before you go. And yet, I wondered if he had really paid attention, if he had somehow believed he was invulnerable, a special exception to Mother Nature's unforgiving ways.

I think that's why I came back at first, to confront him, maybe even to scold him for his reckless choices. He was always the one who looked out for me, and now I'm standing here, at the very spot where he lost his life.

An endless stretch of white stretches out before me, the snow swirling over the ice in lazy drifts. This is where we used to play, back when the lake was our winter playground during Christmas break. When the ice was thick, the snow still light, and we would tie sleds around our waists, racing across the frozen surface as fast as our rubber-soled boots could carry us. Laughter would echo through the air, making it seem as if we were the only two souls in our own magical world.

I take a few tentative steps onto the lake. It feels solid under my shoes, the snow crunching under my feet as I make my way across. It isn't thin, it isn't melting, so why did it shatter under him? I walk faster out to the centre, waiting to feel the ice bend under the pressure of my weight, but it holds firm.

I remember how he and I used to battle all sorts of creatures on this ice. Evil snowmen didn't stand a chance against the sticks we'd find along the shoreline. We'd duck behind snowdrifts, laughing as Dad launched snowballs our way, and Mum would chase us until we were caught in her warm bear hugs.

We used to rush back to the house after a day on the ice and huddle in the warm kitchen, our cheeks red and snowsuits damp. Dad would scold us to pick up the wet clothes that inevitably ended up on the tiled floor. Mum's famous hot chocolate would steam in our faces as we recounted the days adventures with the eagerness of our youth. There was this one mug my brother always kept for himself, the one with a painted trout and a handle shaped like a fish tail. I suppose I can finally use it now.

I wipe my face with my gloved hands, the wet stains from tears soaking through the fabric. My knees sink into the snow as I double over, howling in my overwhelming grief. He is gone. Just like that girl from my childhood, he was here one moment and then, just vanished from my life forever.

I continue to kneel as the sun begins to set on the horizon, its orange rays casting a melancholic glow over the snow. The temperature slowly begins to drop around me, a shiver working its way through my body as tears start to freeze on my cheeks. In the distance, the trees creak and sway in the biting wind. My hair ruffles in the cold air as I look up at the fading sun and sigh. It's time to head back home.

Shards of Gratitude

KYLIE GROSE

'I hate my life!' and then—smash—shards of mirror rained reflective daggers. Luckily, Krystal had forgotten to pick up the towels and clothes from the last week. The shards laid there like a sea of broken reflections, some reflecting the ugly tiles on the wall, and some reflecting her face, giving her face a distorted look. One piece remained on the wall; she was drawn to trace her finger around the outside edge of the piece. She closed her eyes and imagined if this piece could reflect another version of herself, Krystal with a better job than her brother …

She opened her eyes, and she was standing in front of a mirror, a complete mirror, and she was dressed in a dress suit! 'What happened?'

She wasn't sure if she said this aloud or in her head when another very well-dressed lady walked in and exclaimed, 'Yeah, I know right! Congratulations! CEO! You totally deserve it!' Krystal noted a hint of sarcasm in her voice.

CEO! Of what? She ventured outside the bathroom into a marble-tiled hall. She hesitantly wandered into an office that was about the size of her apartment with a stunning view of the Brisbane River and city. A guy walked in behind her, shoulders slumped, ruffled hair, a slightly dishevelled suit. He looked surprised to see Krystal.

'Oh, sorry, I haven't packed my stuff up yet, I've been … at lunch, yeah, that sounds good … at lunch. I'll be packed by the end of the day.'

'Ah, it's ok, no rush. I was just …'

'Checking out the view, I know …' he said, as though he knew her.

'Don't worry, you can move in first thing tomorrow … I'll be … gone.'

At that, Krystal started to walk towards the door and noticed his name tag—*Shaun*—and a photo of him and the sarcastic lady she met in the bathroom.

Krystal ran to the bathroom … This was not what she was expecting. She rubbed her finger in the spot where the shard was on her smashed mirror, closed her eyes and was never so grateful to be back in the bathroom with ugly tiles and a smashed mirror.

The big CEO job wasn't really what she imagined; too much pressure and stressful relationships. Krystal decided she was quite settled in her current job, so she started to think of another scenario, perhaps … no brother … sorry, Shaun.

She picked up another shard, placed it on the wall, closed her eyes and …

Krystal found herself in a very spacious bathroom, then walked out into a very spacious unit with a view to die for! She thought she'd call her mum. Her mum's number was one of two numbers saved, but it was under her mum's first name, not as *Mum*. That was strange …

'Oh, you finally decided to call me? Be quick, I'm about to go to dinner with Shaun at some fancy restaurant here in Paris.'

'Mum?'

'Oh, it's Mum now, when did that change?'

'Mum? Who's Shaun? How long have you been in Paris?'

'Don't you mean *how can you afford to be in Paris?* Well, my new boyfriend, Shaun, has family here, so he asked me to join him. Not like you, heading to the big city. I have no other family …' Her mum hung up, her voice quivering.

Krystal went back to her fancy bathroom and decided that being a spoilt only-child wasn't really all it was cracked up to be.

Krystal picked up another shard—she had always imagined a life with a husband and the average 2.2 children, so she placed the shard back on the wall roughly where it seemed to fit, rubbed her finger on the outside edge and closed her eyes …

Screams … a small child holding her legs … a man shouting from upstairs, 'Where's my ironed shirt? Hun … can you please have a look? It's a big interview today, I have a good feeling about this one!'

Krystal opened her eyes. The little one holding her legs must have been about two years old. He was looking up at her, holding an empty bottle. He had red, swollen eyes from crying. There was quite the brawl going on upstairs between two siblings, and the man who was calling for his shirt seemed oblivious to it.

She went to the kitchen to fill the bottle, the toddler managing to keep hold of her legs. She noticed a picture on the fridge with a colourful squiggle and the name *Shaun*. She filled the bottle with cold water and returned it to Shaun's plump, tiny hands. It went straight to his mouth, he took a sip, then promptly threw it to the ground. 'Yuck, me want juju!'

'Hun, any luck with the shirt? Hun?'

Krystal wondered if this man was any better than the .2 screaming for juju. She decided to go back to the bathroom … trying to unclench .2's arms from her legs.

She had decided very quickly this time that she was incredibly grateful for her single life with no children. Although she will play with her brother's kids sometime soon, they were so quiet, playful and calm.

Krystal imagined a few more scenarios with each shard she picked up. They never seemed any better than where she was in life right now. She realised her brother, Shaun, wasn't too bad of a brother. Her mum was trying to give her independence, but going on a cruise with her brother and his family at Christmas without an invite was a bit harsh.

Even though there were a few jagged edges, some small pieces missing, all-in-all Krystal was grateful for her family, friends and life in general.

Strawberry Gumboots

MILLIE MAE PEDDER

I don't cry easily, just ask my best friend Katie. When I do cry, it feels like the rain falls just because of me. Everything is soaked by the sky's tears. My raincoat only does so much, and water pools in my gumboots. It's too soggy.

What am I doing out here? I'm not in the mood to play, all I can do is think about stuff. My raincoat squeaks with every movement, and the material catches my skin. My bucket hat squeezes my head. I'm getting a headache just like last time.

I'm staying with Dad this week. I stare at the droplet-stained window of his office. Was it last year that I would sit by that window and watch the droplets as they race down the glass? I no longer watch them race. Instead, I look past them at Dad typing away at his computer. He is always at his computer. He says it's work that he *must* do, but he doesn't look like he's having fun. The rain beats down on my hands and shins. I would ask Dad to come play with me. But every time, the answer is the same. 'Maybe later,' or, 'Not right now.'

Mum is the same.

I don't ask anymore. They'll notice soon. I hope.

I'm turning eight on Friday. Katie says her parents take her to water parks every birthday. She is so lucky. I've never been to one, not even when Mum and Dad were together. I empty my gumboots again and remember the last time we were a family.

Mum had come home from work on Christmas Eve. I clutched a few books and pens in my arms. I was smiling, hopeful.

'Mummy? Can you draw with me?'

She slumped over the counter and sighed. 'Why can't you just be a good girl and clean your room or unpack the dishwasher for once?' she mumbled. 'I hate coming home when nothing's been done.'

From then on, I always made sure my room was tidy and the dishwasher was unpacked. Because I hated how I felt when it wasn't. How *she* made me feel when it wasn't. I don't think she noticed. The next day was Christmas. Under the tree was my poorly wrapped present.

It's … A shoebox. Inside was something pink and rubbery. Gumboots. Just what every *grown-up* girl wants …

They had a strawberry pattern and were one size too small. But I couldn't appear ungrateful—my parents were always working. I plastered a smile on my face, and it seemed to have convinced them ever since.

Dinner was different that night. I can't remember how or why they started screaming. It was Christmas Day. A time when families were supposed to come together—not *this*. I had grabbed the drawing I made from our *last* family holiday. It was Sydney, Bondi Beach. I crept toward the dining room, wincing at every creak in the floorboard. Mum threw her wine glass and it shattered against the wall, leaving the carpet stained red and glittering with shards of glass.

I gasped and my parents' heads snapped toward me. I stepped forward and stood as tall as I could. I was going to help, cheer them up, fix it.

'I—I did this, remember?' I held the picture up with clammy hands. I had used real seashells and sand to make the beach come alive again. My chest puffed out a bit like a kookaburra. I won the end-of-year drawing competition with my art. Even beating Katie, who was always perfect. I *knew* they were proud.

Neither smiled. There was no glimmer of pride in their eyes. Water welled in my eyes, and a hole opened in my chest.

Mum spoke first. 'I'm leaving.'

The hole grew so big it swallowed me. My drawing floated to the floor as I clutched my hands over my chest. What was wrong with me? What did I do? What *could* I do? It was getting hard to breathe. I was drowning, even though I was gasping in air. Dad said nothing and went to his office for the rest of the night. I stared out the droplet-stained window as the lights of Mum's car vanished in the distance. Wattle and bottlebrush branches whipped the air, caught in a violent whirlwind.

I'm still wearing those strawberry gumboots. They're still too tight and still hurt my toes, but they remind me of how things were before. When we were a family. Is that why I don't ask for new ones? Am I just too attached? Or am I already enough of a burden?

It isn't fair.

I watch my reflection ripple in a puddle. My brows knit together, and my nose scrunches up. You're meant to get cold from being in the rain. So why does my body feel like a boiling pot about to burst? Heat continues to rise through me. I want to scream, but my throat is closed. My body shakes, and my fists clench. It hurts as my nails dig into my palms. I stare at my reflection. I hate her. She can't even help the ones I love. As I draw back my leg, itchy cotton fabric irritates my shin's flesh. I kick my reflection, and splashes scatter the image like glass. My happy memories fade and sour, dissolving into the sky's tears.

Another Day in Hell

MAEVE WILSON

6 a.m. came too soon.

The screech of the alarm serenaded the new hour, joining the chorus of birds that had taken up residence in the gutter above the bedroom window—they had been wailing nonstop since the crack of dawn.

Jack rolled over with a groan, not yet ready to open his eyes to the bright morning sun already forcing its way through the cracks in the blinds. Eyes still closed, he slapped his hand across the top of his nightstand, hoping to stop the piercing sounds; but it was too late. There was a fast-paced rap against the bedroom door, flung open before he could answer. Two small silhouettes stood upon the threshold.

The taller of the two was the first to speak, 'Daddy! You're awake!'

'Get up, Dad! We want breakfast!'

'Go to the kitchen, I'll be up in a minute.' Jack groaned as he dragged himself into a sitting position.

The sound of giggles and the patter of feet faded down the hallway. Jack looked down to his left. Despite the commotion, Amy was undisturbed; soft snores revealing her unaltered unconsciousness. She didn't usually snore, she'd apologised to Jack last night; knowing that her sinus infection was likely keeping him from getting a good night's sleep for the last few nights. Jack had told her not to worry about him and to just focus on getting better, but truth have it, Jack was starting to get annoyed at the lack of sleep and even more annoyed at having to deal with making breakfast even after he'd barely slept.

The TV was already blaring by the time Jack made his way out to the kitchen. The girls still didn't know how to use the remote properly, so instead of their usual morning cartoons, the news channel was still playing.

'*Reports from Afghanistan say that the Taliban has discovered a secret girls' school operating in a residential hideout. The school was allegedly educating approximately 18 young women, none of whom have been seen since—*'

'*—and you're watching Disney Channel!*'

The girls cheered at the change of channel. Jack couldn't understand why they always put such depressing stuff on in the morning. Did news stations want people to have a bad day?

'Girls, go put your uniforms on while I get your breakfast ready.'

'But Dad, they're dirty.'

Shit. Jack remembered Amy asking him to wash and dry the girls' uniforms before bed last night, but he'd forgotten. He didn't know why Amy even trusted him with the task; she was always complaining that he didn't sort the colours correctly and he was always somehow using the wrong setting. This day was going from bad to worse.

He couldn't believe it; he was going to be late for work. After fighting his way through school traffic, city traffic was the last thing he wanted to deal with, and he was already dreading work. He had a big meeting planned for the day and was trying to practice what he wanted to say but the honking of car horns and drone of the radio was incessant.

'*Unemployment is at a high while many suffer from the pressures of the cost of living cri—*' Jack switched to aux—he was sick of the constant negativity.

The meeting had gone well. Upper management took his suggestions on board and Jack felt good. Good, but not great. He had wanted to get some more work done but was struggling to concentrate; it always happened at this time of day. Around 3 p.m. the sun would begin to slide down the horizon, reflecting off the mirrored glass of the neighbouring buildings and shining almost directly into Jack's office, the glare making him squint. He had gotten most of what he needed to get done and was dreading his next foray into the metropolitan traffic. He had told Amy when she was pregnant with their first that he didn't want to live too far from the city, but she insisted they needed somewhere bigger, somewhere they wouldn't 'outgrow'. But now, instead of a quick train trip to and from work, it was a minimum 20-minute drive. *Ah well,* Jack thought, *at least it's cheaper.* Then again, it wasn't like money was that much of an issue.

By the time the clock hit 9 p.m., Jack was exhausted. Just as he left work, Amy called and asked him if he could pick the girls up from after-school care because she was feeling even more sick after her shift. Of course he did it, he'd never have heard the end of it if he hadn't. To make matters worse, by the rate that Amy was recovering, he was probably going to have to do the netball run on the weekend too. *There go my plans to have some beers with the footy tomorrow night*, Jack thought; frustrated he wouldn't be able to decompress properly after his week.

Amy's arm lay across his chest, her breathing still loud and crackling. Jack sighed as he switched off the light, ready to rest himself for another day of hell.

Safe and Sound

Abbey-Lee Stibbard

*T*he school bell rings and I'm the first out of the door. My classmates' parents wait outside but I don't look for mine, I already know dad is not there.

I shove past the people, making an effort to sneak past the boys who like to pick on me, Max and Jake. My once-pink backpack bounces on my back like a turtle's shell as I run down the hill, into the bushland behind the school grounds. I hear water splashing over the rocks and leaves whispering in the wind. It's like the bush welcoming me back. I squeeze through the hole in the fence and push through the overgrowth. It's the entrance to a magical, enchanted land.

'Faye!' my small voice echoes amongst the gum trees.

I see the flowing creek ahead but hear no reply from my imaginary friend. I wonder if she's playing hide and seek. I search behind the trees and peak around each trunk, looking for footprints in the soft dirt below. Frustrated, I walk to the water's edge, take off my black school shoes, and dip my little toes into the creek. I giggle as the cold water tickles my skin. All my worries seem to wash away, it's like nothing can hurt me here in my special place.

A loud 'BOO!' fills the air.

I fall back landing feet up in the shallow water.

'Got you!' Faye exclaims and I burst into laughter, splashing her. Faye throws her long, white hair over her shoulder, her smile playful and comforting. Her shimmering brown dress reflects the colours of the bush around us.

'Nice to see you too,' I say, climbing out of the water. My dress is soaked and covered in mud. It looks less like a school uniform and more like Faye's dress—like the bush has worked its magic on it.

She takes my hand and we skip along the edge of the water, pretending we are explorers. I climb over the rocks and brush against the scratchy bushes until we reach the waterfall.

It's the most beautiful waterfall in the whole wide world! The water falls just above my head and misty spray sprinkles over my face.

'Can we pretend to be ballerinas today? The girls at school are enrolled in dance, but you know how Dad says I'm not allowed,' I say as I take her arm and spin underneath.

'Remember, you can be whatever you want to be,' she replies and balances on one leg in arabesque. I try to copy her, my arms out wide to help me stay upright.

I fall when I hear somebody approaching behind me.

'Oi! Look who it is, our little weirdo friend!' Two boys from my school appear from behind the bushes and walk towards where I sit on the floor. I recognise them immediately: Max and Jake. The boys loom over me, their shadows swallowing me up. The birds stop chirping; the waterfall stops flowing—everything goes still.

'Talking to your invisible friend again?' Jake asks. Max laughs beside him, nudging his elbow to egg him on.

My heart pounds. They're bigger and older than me. But Faye stands beside me and her comforting smile makes me feel protected. She nods at me as though to give me permission to be brave.

'Leave me alone. I'm having fun here!' I exclaim, standing up off the dirt, pretending I'm taller than I am.

The boys both smirk as though they're about to say something cruel, but Faye's light fills me with the bravery to stand up for myself. She is completely invisible to the boys, my secret support.

'Fun in this muddy dump? Weir—'

'You can leave if you don't have anything nice to say,' I interrupt, my voice loud and clear. The look on the boys' faces switches from sneaky to shock. 'This is my place, and I won't let your mean words ruin it.'

The boys exchange looks as though they didn't expect me to speak up so bravely. I felt like I was defending my land.

'Let's just go,' Max states as he drags Jake away. Their footsteps fade off into the bush as Faye gives me a nod of approval and her eyes glimmer with pride.

'Let's get back to your ballet lesson.'

The sun begins to set; the sky becomes warm and golden. The creek no longer glitters and the trees have become dark, scary shadows. My visit to the creek is over and it is time to return to my reality. I put my school bag on my back and Faye holds me in her comforting embrace. We both know what waits for me outside of the bush.

'I'll see you tomorrow,' Faye says, and reminds me: 'You are strong my girl. You are magical.'

I nod as Faye disappears into the darkness. The shadows eat her up and once again, I'm all alone.

I arrive home to the familiar smell of alcohol and mess. Dad lies on the couch asleep; his empty beer bottles are scattered around. The room is dimly lit and the TV plays quietly in the corner. I wish I could open the drawn curtains. At least then the moonlight would shine in and fill the air with something other than sadness.

I tiptoe past the couch, making sure I don't make a sound. I know what will happen if I wake him. His mean words will shoot like arrows and I don't want to be afraid again.

I escape into my bedroom and shut the door behind me. I wrap myself in a blanket and close my eyes. I picture the glittering creek, the golden sun shining onto the waterfall and Faye, the protector of it all.

I feel close to the magic of the creek, the place where my bravery and happiness live. I know morning will soon come and I will be back, safe and sound in my enchanted land.

Breakfast with a View

ZARA TAMMO

*D*eep, dark blue fills the open sky as the light of the stars begin to fade. All is still until I see a glow rise over the ocean on the horizon. Then suddenly, a burst. Glows of orange spread far and wide, as the sun peaks its head up.

I watch as rays beam between patches of green, waking what was once asleep. Calls fill the air, conducting an orchestra of song. Here, the once dark olive leaves turn colours of emerald and lime. The drops that had once clung to the leaves trickle down to the earth below. Where each drop lands dirt spools into mud, while others drip down into the rivers that flow amongst the stone. I watch as small animals wake from their slumber. Then, slowly hop, waddle and skip to the edge of the bank. They take their turns in drinking the water and raise their weary eyes to the skies above.

I move with the river's winds and curves, down the river's edge. I watch as the flora changes from tall trees to shrubs, while the ground fades out of colour. Finally, the river meets its mouth where it opens up wide. Out beyond, I see the sea, where the morning welcomes the light. Now the sky is a bright blue beam, reflecting onto the water beneath and I strain my eyes to see what may lay below.

Splash. A tail flips against the water. Then a fin rises, waving 'hi' to me. A pod moves along, leaving a trace of white against the blue. Their puffs and spurts spray the air and carry in the wind. I shake as the cool water flickers onto me.

Further out, a boat sails. From above, it looks like an animal of the sea, drifting to where the current will take it. The reefs below are the homes of fish, coral and more. They scurry in the seabeds, looking for their next meal. A turtle drifts, like the boat it had neared. Only briefly does its head touch the surface, to have a peak at the skies above.

I make my way back past the gates to the sea and laze about in the sun. I wonder where else my day may take me as I search for a drink. Then off again I go, away from the busy streets. I wander and I wander until I find a land of green grass.

The field spreads as far as the eye can see. Patches mismatch in colour, creating its own portrait on the land. Yellow, dried terrain shows where the sugar cane had once grown. Now, it is rolled in mounds and stacked to look like people in a scene. Its sweet scent carries through the air like a baked cake wafting freshly from an oven.

Another patch sways lightly in the wind. The small, white flowers it holds slowly rock awake. Petals open their arms to the rays of sun and breathe in the air of a new day. A buzz tells me the bees have arrived. They move their way onward in unformed lines and take what they need and leave.

Food, I remember, *I haven't got any food.* I get up and move in search of some food. *Now, where might I find it?* I wonder. I take another look ahead and see some houses in the distance. *Well they may have some food,* I think, and go to see what is there.

I look through the cobblestone streets and over the walls. Then through the bushes to see if anything has fallen. As I turn down another street, I can see the tree I had been looking for. The tree. The big tree. The one filled with my favourite fruit … blueberries.

I peek around the corner to see if anyone is home. Then I listen as hard as I can. No-one seems to be there, so I make my move. I hop past the fence and over to the bush. Quickly and quietly, I take as many berries as possible. Then a noise rises from the kitchen.

'Mum, look, it's back,' a child says.

'No.' I try to stop him.

'Shoo, get out of here you foul…' the mother's voice calls. She walks outside with a broom in her hand.

I take the berries and move as fast as I can. I go back through the town, past the fields and along the streets. I stop and catch my breath, back at the sea. I look and feel its calm. Oh, what a marvellous morning this has been.

As I make my way back to my home, I think of the stories I will tell. To see the little ones with their excitement and reactions. I get to the riverbank and fly back up in the air. I see my babies, each calling back to me.

'I have your food here,' I say. Each take their portion of the blueberries. 'I have flown far and wide to find these. Just wait till you hear about my morning.'

Maya, the Old Man, and the Whale

JESSICA LANE

The sand was cool beneath Maya's feet, untouched by the amber glow slowly saturating the horizon. Light cascaded over the blue and silver shadows like ice melting upon warmth, gently dissolving the night.

She took a deep breath in, a slow count of one, two, three … *exhale*.

For the past five years, Maya had followed this ritual every morning, always in awe of how each dawn offered something new. Her father had nurtured this ritual. As a marine biologist, he instilled in her a deep understanding of the delicate balance within the ecosystem and how it mirrored their own lives. He taught her to observe the subtle changes that each day brought and to find marvel in the small, everyday moments.

'Like the ever-shifting tide, we too are in a constant state of change,' he would say. 'And the best way to journey far is to move with the current, not against it.'

As the sand began to warm under the morning sun, Maya finished her stretches, then lifted her kayak and paddle. The sea was calm, its flat surface transformed into a shimmering mirror. Her paddle glided through the water, each stroke propelling her farther out to sea. The breeze stole the sleep from her eyes as the sun began to kiss her skin. It had almost completely risen over the horizon now, casting a glow across the sea ahead of her.

Suddenly, less than 500 metres away, a violent thrashing broke the tranquillity. Maya squinted, trying to make out what was disturbing the calm water. Her heart skipped a beat. There, tangled in a string of yellow buoys, a young humpback whale struggled against a shark net.

Without hesitation, Maya paddled toward the whale, her heart racing. Her father's words echoed in her head: 'One small action can ripple any tide.' Fear gripped her, but the thought of turning back never crossed her mind. She was needed here.

As she neared the whale, she saw its sheer size up close—the creature was enormous, powerful, and terrified. Its fluke slammed against the water, sending waves toward her kayak, threatening to capsize it. Maya's hands shook, but her resolve hardened. She grabbed the knife strapped to her belt and, despite the danger, paddled closer.

Her vision tunnelled, focusing on the net wrapped around the whale's body. The rope was tangled tightly around its fins, cutting into its flesh. She couldn't jump into the water—it was too risky with the whale thrashing in fear.

Leaning over the kayak, Maya stretched her shaking arms out as far as she could and began sawing through the ropes. The knife was small, the ropes thick, and every second felt like a lifetime. The loud thump of her heartbeat pounded in her ears, drowning out everything but the whale's cries.

Each cut, a desperate attempt to free the whale, her breath caught with each successful slice. She watched as the whale's desperate movements weakened; she was running out of time. The whale was growing weaker with each passing minute.

In a moment too fast to fathom, the steadfast protection of the kayak was swept from beneath her as Maya was thrown deep beneath the tumultuous surface.

Panic surged in her chest as the cold depths swallowed her. She thrashed, trying to find which way was up. A rope had coiled around her ankle, dragging her down alongside the whale. She fumbled for her knife, but it had disappeared into the murky depths.

Her lungs burned as she fought for air. She forced herself to stop thrashing and think—her father's words once again grounding her: One, two, three ... *exhale*. Slowly, Maya's mind cleared. As her heart rate slowed, she reached down, desperately feeling for the rope tangled around her ankle. Her fingers grasped at nothing, and her vision began to fade into darkness.

Suddenly, a firm grip seized her shoulder and hauled her upwards in a current of confusing salvation.

Maya broke through the surface, coughing and spluttering as she gulped down the precious salty air. The world around was a blur of frenzied movement and spray, her lungs alive with the grateful burn of breathing.

'You alright, kid?'

Beside her, a spluttering old man bobbed in the churning water. His faded-yellow coat clung to his waterlogged frame as he too gasped for air. Without waiting for an answer, he hauled her towards his small boat, a safe distance from the whale's thrashes.

Maya laid there for a moment, catching her breath. Her eyes stinging from the saltwater, her body trembling from the cold. She glanced back at the whale, which had momentarily stopped struggling, its enormous body floating limply in the water. She knew they were running out of time.

'We have to help it,' Maya croaked, her voice hoarse.

The old man nodded; his face lined with determination. 'We don't have much time, it's only young and very weak. Grab that knife from the tackle box.'

Together, they inched closer to the whale, Maya's hands quivering as she gripped the knife. The old man steadied her, their breath ragged with urgency. She sliced through the ropes, each cut a desperate prayer. The whale thrashed violently, nearly overturning the boat, but they pressed on, driven by hope.

Finally, the last rope fell away. The whale was free.

But it didn't move.

The great creature floated, its chest barely rising. The light in its eyes had dimmed.

Maya let out a small cry as the lifeless body floated still in the water. It was free ... but it was too late. Tears welled in her eyes as she watched the massive creature drift slowly away from the boat.

Maya and the old man watched in silence, their hearts heavy with sorrow. From below, they saw the mother whale approaching. She nudged the youth, waiting wilfully for its response. After minutes of unnatural stillness, the whale let out a mournful cry, breaching the surface one last time before diving deep into the ocean, leaving only ripples.

Maya wiped her tears, hands trembling, as the old man's voice broke through the silence, thick with grief.

'These nets ... they don't save lives. They just take them,' he whispered, his weathered face streaked with sorrow. 'Someone has to stop this.'

Maya's chest tightened, the weight of helplessness crushing her, but within it burned a fierce resolve. She looked into his tear-filled eyes, her own heart shattered, and whispered back, 'I will.'

Plastic HOPE

Jazmin Heather

*K*ristin stared at the heirloom bracelet, placed in her hand by a silver-haired woman she barely knew. She wasn't sure she could do what was asked—give it away. Wasn't sure about hospital policy. But having now heard the tales (the bracelet had been to London, Rio and Nairobi to name a few), Kristin couldn't refuse. The woman was terminal; she wanted its stories continued. So she took the stairs back to floor three, the bracelet a sighing weight in her pocket.

A little girl on floor three sat quietly on her bed, spinning her own bracelet around. The elastic was fraying, split ends poking out. Its plastic beads clacked delicately, distracting her from the humming machines and hushed voices.

The Make-Your-Own-Bracelet kit had included a variety of beads. There were bright neon stars, beads plain and patterned, beads resembling fruit slices and smiley faces, and exactly 107 alphabet beads. Josie's bracelet held a wild combination, including four letters. It was these four Josie fiddled with most, moving anxious fingers from **H** to **O** to **P** to **E** and back again.

She tensed when a hand touched her head. Well, not her head but one of many silk scarves Josie now owned. She hated them. They reminded her of baby bibs, all tied behind her neck. But the first time she'd tried one, her mother had glowed, delighted.

Josie had been delighted by a shaved head; the hair falling out was itchy. She pictured her and her dad, sitting side by side in front of the large mirror. 'We're in the baldie club,' she'd said, and he'd laughed.

'... back tomorrow, okay?'

Josie feigned attention, nodding and smiling like she was supposed to, but she pulled at the four letters. Too hard.

Beads flew everywhere, bouncing, tapping, rolling on the floor.

Leaping off the bed, she scrambled after them, looking for the four letters in particular.

'Josie, it's okay.' Her mother's voice rose. 'You get to go home tonight, Josie. Home. Please.'

Josie's shoulders fell even while she was lifted to her feet and tugged along, leaving the beads behind.

Henry watched Josie leave from the door of his room, her tutu lifting lightly with each step. She turned back to look at him before crossing two fingers over one, holding out her hand for him to see. *Double luck*, they called it. At ten, he felt each of the four years between them deeply. He knew they were neighbours on purpose, neither having siblings nor lots of family, but he'd never minded the set-up. Josie was always destined to be his little sister.

He turned wide, brown eyes to the nurse, Kristin, standing outside. She caught him looking and smiled a little.

'Should we fix Josie's bracelet?'

He nodded solemnly. The bracelet was Josie's favourite.

They worked quickly, filling a plastic cup. When every corner of Josie's room was scoured, Henry realised their problem and frowned. 'Is there something to put the beads on?'

Kristin paused, considering. 'I might have something.' She smiled at him bigger. 'Head back to your room, and I'll bring it?'

Henry nodded. His room next door was a boy version of Josie's—all superhero posters and scattered Pokémon cards. Someone would bring lunch any minute, but until then, he was tired. He ached deeper than his bones.

'Henry?' Kristin's voice woke him. A tray of food sat on the table, but he wasn't hungry. Being sick sometimes stole all the space in his stomach.

'Did you find anything?' It came out breathless; the air felt a bit thick.

'I did. Something really special.' Kristin came in and handed him his oxygen tube, getting it situated before she made a note on his clipboard.

He held out a hand. 'Can I see it?' Kristin pulled the bracelet from her pocket and placed it in his palm. It was silver and delicate and nice. Henry grinned up at her. 'Fancy,' he said.

Kristin nodded. 'There was an older lady who asked me to give it away.'

'She doesn't want it?'

'She said the bracelet deserved more adventures.' Kristin pretended to frown, placing a hand around her chin, finger tapping her cheek in thought. 'I wasn't sure what to do with it at first, but what do you think? Will that work for Josie?'

Henry furrowed his brow, pretending with her. 'It'll do, Kristin.' He caught her smile as she turned away, and it made his own bigger.

'I'll bring the beads in so you can string it back together,' she said.

Three coerced bites later, Henry was concentrating hard. They tried to recall the exact order of the beads, arranging them next to each other on the tray, framing **H-O-P-E** the way he remembered: a pink neon star on one side and a smiley face on the other.

One by one, the beads skimmed down the silver bracelet as he filled it from one end. His hands were shaky by the time he was done.

'It looks beautiful, Henry,' Kristin said.

He nodded. 'Better than before.' He ate two more bites before double crossing his fingers and falling asleep.

Kristin watched as Henry showed the bracelet to Josie, her big, blue eyes going wide as she gasped in the genuine, dramatic fashion only little girls can manage. Josie held out her arm, and Henry carefully slipped the bracelet over her small fist, not needing to unclasp it.

'I'll never take it off,' she swore. Henry nodded—with a solemnity that far surpassed his age or station—and wrapped her in a hug, whispering to her.

Kristin walked in, hating to break them up. 'It's time for treatment, Josie.' She never asked kids if they were ready; it broke her, how bravely they lied.

Josie held up her wrist, beaming. 'Henry fixed it! With a real silver bracelet.' She spun around the **H** and **O** and **P** and **E**, plastic beads tapping and clacking along the hundred-year-old bracelet with stories yet to tell.

Milton Keynes UK
Ingram Content Group UK Ltd.
UKHW032051201124
451474UK00005B/282